Dirt Simple Harmonica

by Phil Duncan

Audio Contents

1	Example A: Hole 4 Blow/draw	17	Example 4: Holes 3, 4
2	Example B: Single Tone, Holes 4 - 7	18	Mary Ann
3	Example 1: The C note	19	Down in the Valley
4	Example 2: Holes 4, 5, 6	20	Joyful, Joyful
5	Some Folks Do	21	The Sloop John B.
6	Boil the Cabbage Down	22	Oh, Shenandoah
7	Oh, When the Saints	23	Example 5: Holes 7, 8, 9, 10
8	Jingle Bells	24	Scarborough Fair
9	For He's a Jolly Good Fellow	25	Lonesome Valley
10	Kum Ba Yah	26	Aura Lee
11	Michael, Row the Boat Ashore	27	Silent Night
12	Example 3: C scale, Holes 4, 5, 6, 7	28	Amazing Grace
13	On Top of Old Smokey	29	All Through the Night
14	Lullaby and Good Night	30	Home on the Range
15	Joy to the World	31	Walking Boogie
16	Home, Sweet Home		

1. Examples A & B are played once. Examples 1 thru 5 are repeated 3x times.

2. All tunes/songs are played once without accompaniment. Then after an intro of four (4) measures, the music is repeated 3x times with accompaniment.

www.melbay.com/30474BCDEB

1 2

Visit us on the Web at www.melbay.com — E-mail us at email@melbay.com

Contents

TO THE STUDENT

The harmonica, also known as mouth organ, French harp, tin sandwich and a variety of other names was developed in Germany in the early 19th century. People have enjoyed playing this instrument seemingly forever.

It is popular because it is ***simple*** to play and ***easy*** to transport. If challenged by other musical instruments, this is the instrument to play. Even for the practiced musician, this book can be extremely helpful.

The music and instruction presented requires little or no previous musical experience.

Three things necessary to play:

1. Have a *10-hole diatonic harmonica, key of C*
2. Able to breathe, exhale and inhale
3. Able to pucker/purse the lips

Yes, that is it! You are ready to play the harmonica. *It is as easy as* **1, 2, 3**!

In just a few pages this book will explore the skills of exhaling and inhaling air "*through*" the harmonica mouth piece, ***'ONE HOLE'* at a time**. This book is based on playing melodies. Most of the tunes presented in this book are well known.

The harmonica is an ear instrument; the mouthpiece is in between the lips while playing, listening is necessary. The harmonica will train the ear to hear what is being played. Playing this instrument will automatically develop music listening skills.

Playing the instrument is achieved by simply learning the tunes or songs either using the musical notes, the tablature or a combination of both. After progressing through each tune or song, use the audio to help perfect your solo presentation.

Included in the written music are chord symbols for accompaniment, such as guitar.

Some of the best music is *Americana Music*, sometimes referred to as *American Folk Music*. These are timeless melodies. This is the music that is presented in this book. This book highlights this original form of American musical heritage. Enjoy these wonderful tunes and become part of this great American heritage. Playing these tunes is a way to own a piece of American folk lore.

Let's begin.

For a more complete study of the diatonic harmonica and its possibilities, Mel Bay's "*Deluxe Harmonica Book*" and audio, for the blues style, Mel Bay's "*Easiest Blues Harp Book*" is available.

HOLDING THE HARMONICA

(1) With the numbers on top, hold the 10-hole harmonica in the "V" of the left hand between the first finger and thumb (See below). (2) The right hand cups around the back of the harmonica and the left hand. This should create a sound chamber behind the harmonica. This closed chamber will "warm" the sound of the harmonica.

HAND VIBRATO

You can "*warm*" the sound further by using your right hand to create a wavering tone called "Vibrato." (1) The heels of the hands stay in contact (See below) and (2) the right hand moves back and forth steadily while blowing/drawing. The right hand covering then uncovering the back of the harmonica changes the sound slightly. Increase this movement of the right hand, (Open, close, open, close) the "*vibrato*" will sound faster.

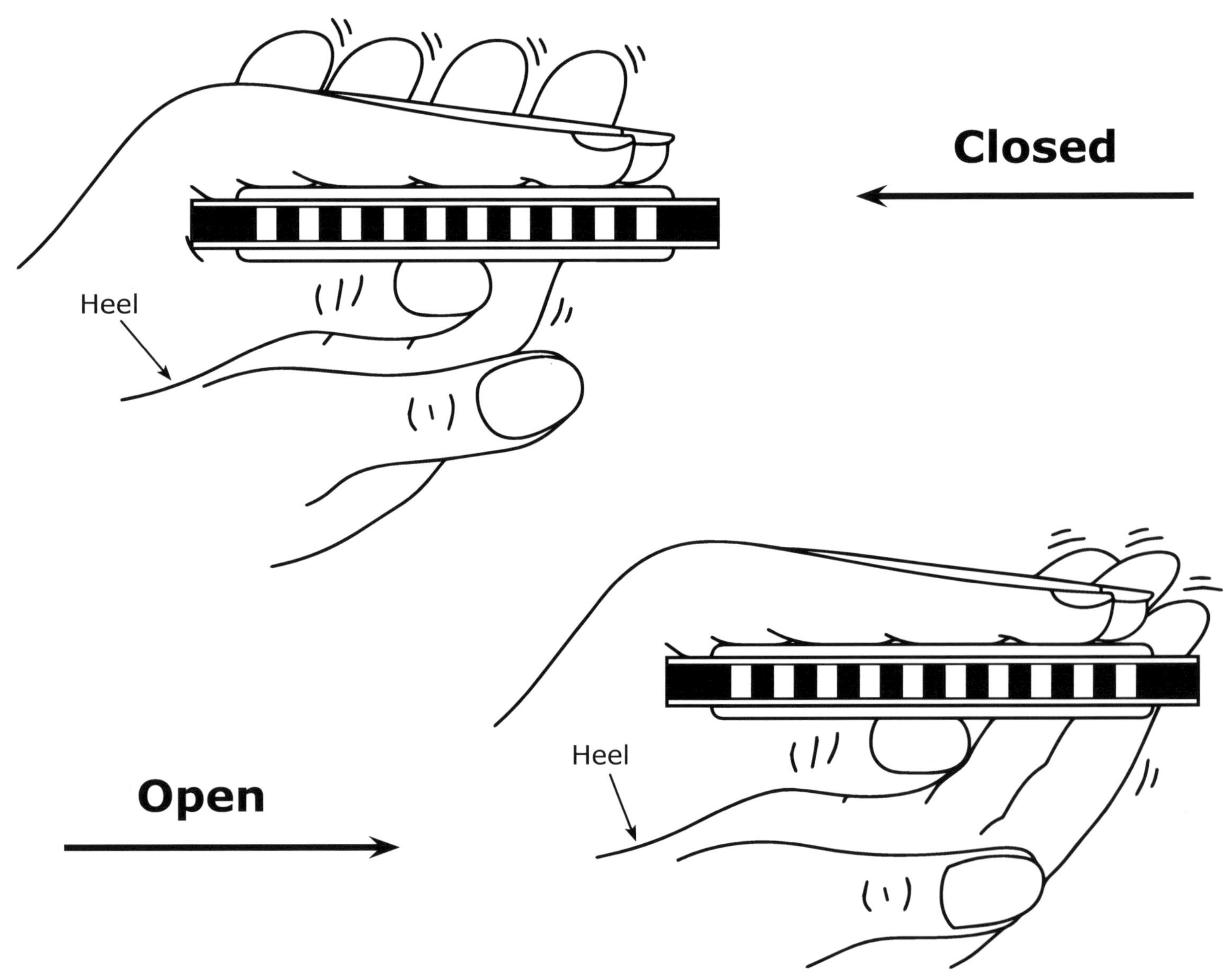

TABLATURE: ARROWS, NUMBERS, & LETTERS

BLOWING/EXHALING

1. Arrows pointing up indicate: ↑ Exhale/**BLOW** into the single numbered hole.
2. "***UPPER CASE***" letters are ***BLOW TONES***. **LARGE NUMBERS** equal ***BLOW***.

drawing/inhaling

3. Arrows pointing down mean: ↓ inhale/**draw** air from a single numbered hole.
4. "***lower case***" letters are ***draw tones***. "**small numbers**" equal **draw**.

OVERVIEW OF THE HARMONICA

Blowing (Exhaling) = ↑ drawing (inhaling) = ↓

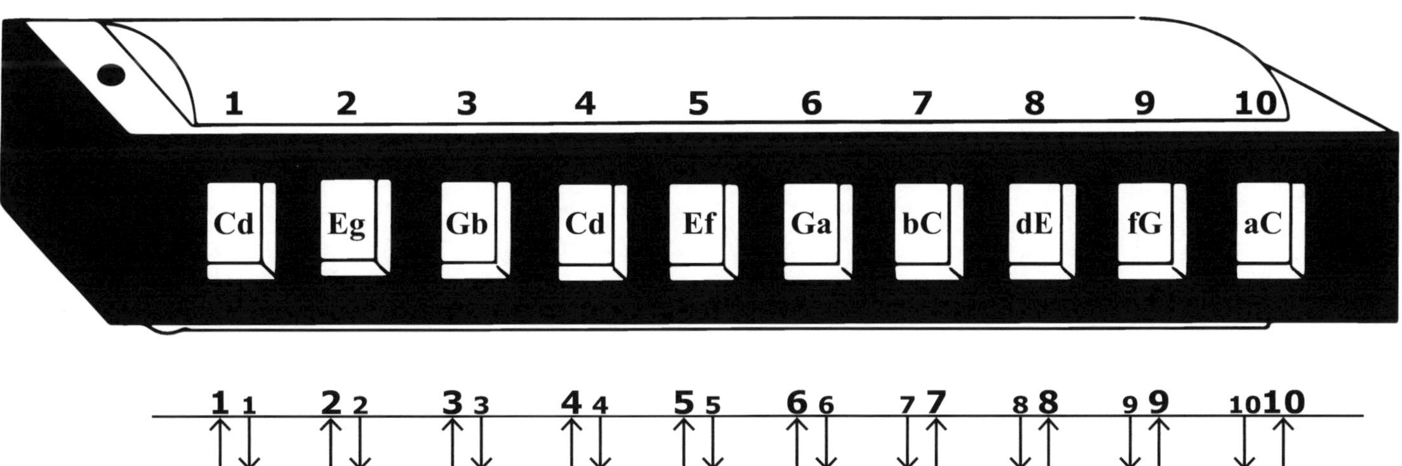

The harmonica shown above is the 10-hole instrument offering 20 different notes, blow and draw, to produce almost three (3) octaves (8 notes/tones equal one octave) of sound. The first and the last notes or tones of the octave are the same letters. Holes 1, 4, 7, and 10 are BLOW C tones. They are an octave apart.

BREATHING '*THROUGH*' THE HARMONICA

The harmonica is the ***ONLY* instrument** that is played by breathing in and out through the instrument. So, simply, just breathe. This may even create healthier lungs. It is a fun breathing machine.

Blowing/exhaling, then drawing/inhaling air through the same hole produces a different tone. Notice below the arrows showing the air flow in for '**C**' and coming out for '**d**' of hole 4.

Please note that air can build up in the lungs, release it through the nose.

Example A:

This larger mouth piece illustration is easier to see. Purse or pucker the lips to create the single sound, moving air into or out of only one hole at a time. (See page 7)

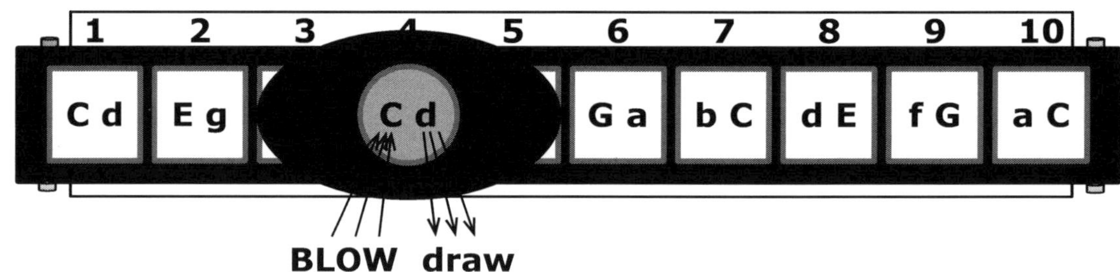

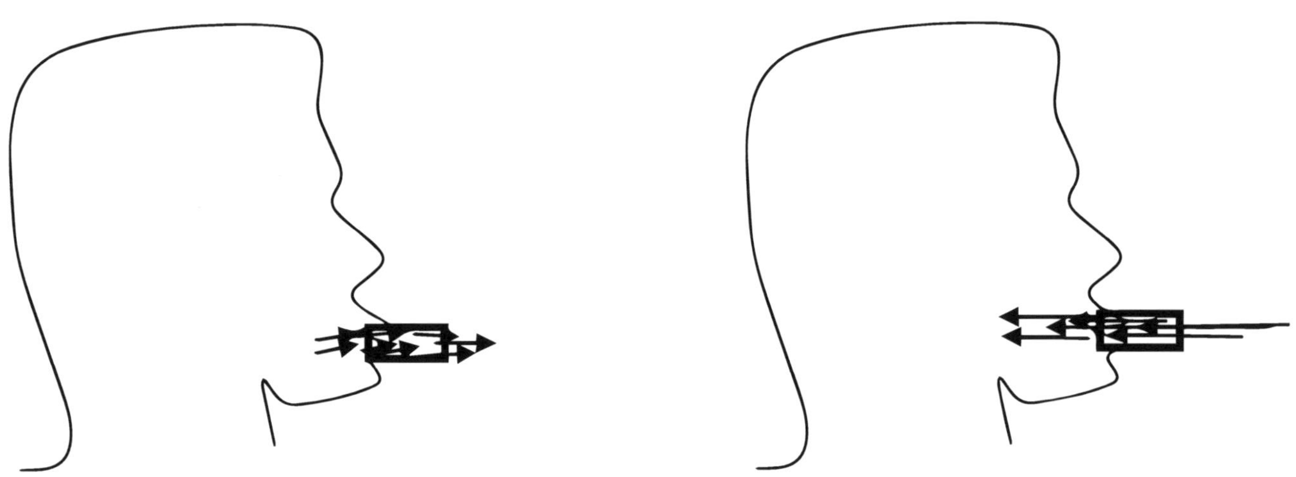

BLOWING Air (Exhale) **drawing air (inhale)**

PLAYING A SINGLE TONE

Whistling, blowing air through a soda straw using pursing or puckering lips or sipping/ inhaling something very hot into the mouth through the lips describes the embouchure (position) of the mouth and lips against the harmonica mouthpiece. This is called '***Lip Blocking***.'

The sides of the lips '**block**' the *adjacent* holes from sounding, creating a single tone in a specific hole. The upper and lower lips seal any air escaping over or under the hole. Move puckered lips to engage other single holes, blowing or drawing in each respective hole. (See illustration below) Blow or draw lightly, like keeping a feather afloat.

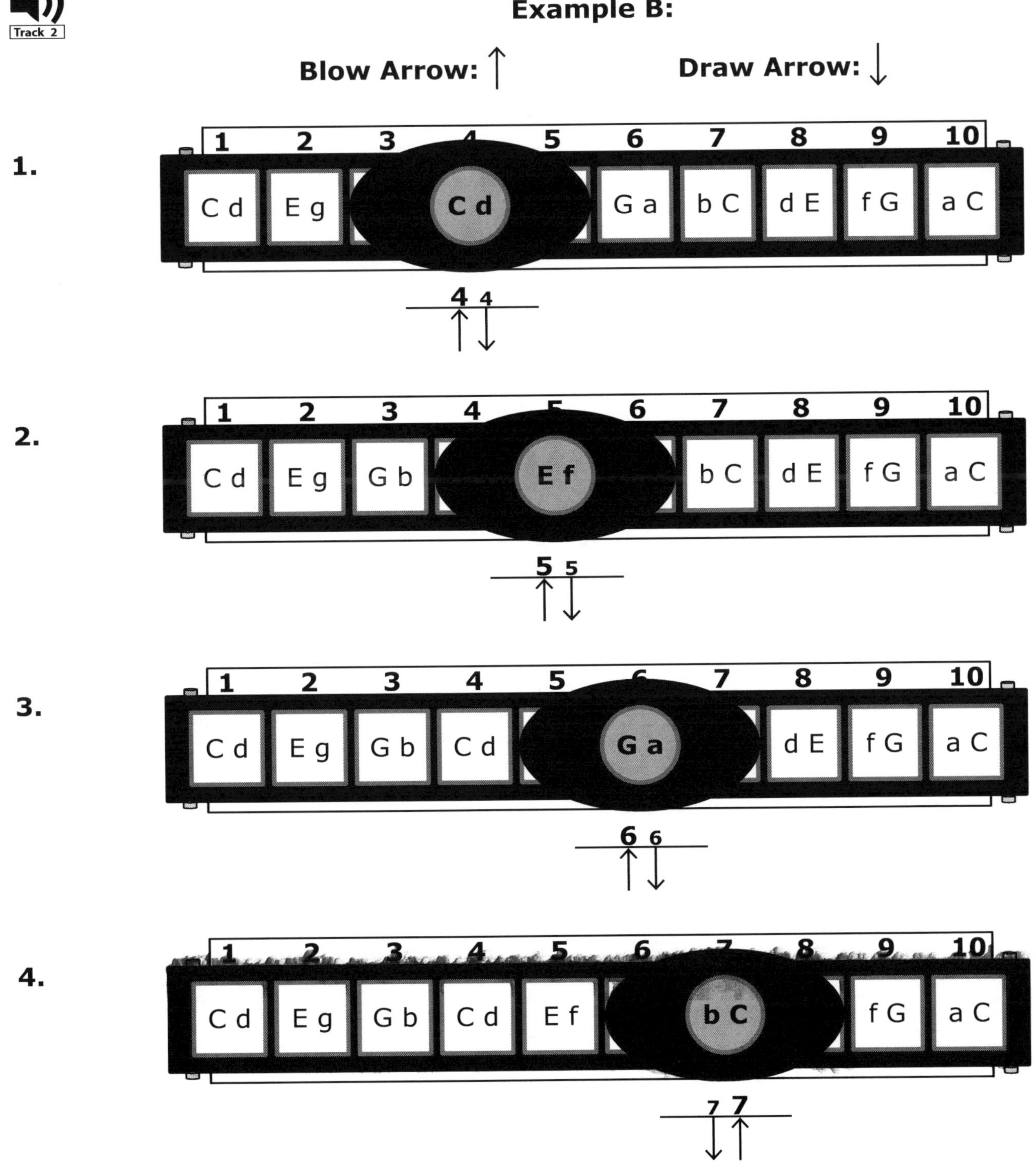

BASIC MUSICAL INFORMATION

A musical staff is 5 horizontal lines creating 4 spaces. Example:

The Staff begins with a Treble Clef Sign: 𝄞 music's upper sound indicator.

Added short lines below/above the musical staff are called "*ledger lines*." An example is Middle C (See next page).

The vertical lines on the horizontal staff lines are measure bars:

These measure bar lines separate the notes into groups of three, four or more counts per measure. The double bar lines (thick line/thin line) start or stop the musical notation. Add two dots on the 2nd and 3rd spaces and they become a repeat sign:

Musical Values/Rhythm

1. **Whole note**: four (**4**) counts; only *one* whole note per measure. (𝅝)
2. **Half notes**: two (**2**) counts; two half notes per measure. (𝅗𝅥)
3. **Quarter notes**: one (**1**) count; four (4) quarter notes per measure. (♩)
4. **Eighth notes**: one-half (**½**) count; eight (8) eighth notes per measure. (♪)

The above note values can extend sound using a dot except the whole note:
1. **Dotted-half notes** (**3** counts) (𝅗𝅥.)
2. **Dotted-quarter notes** (**1½** count) (♩.)

These values keep the rhythm even and steady

Rests – Silence is an equally important part of the music.
1. **Quarter Rest** = one (**1**) count (𝄽)
2. **Half Rest** = two (**2**) counts (𝄼)
3. **Whole Rest** = complete measure (𝄻)

Definitions of curved lines:

1. **Slurs**: Curved line of two 'different' pitches using one syllable. Both notes will sound.
2. **Tie**: Curved line extends the length of the single pitch or note's value.

The tablature, arrows, letters and numbers will help to find the correct sound.

MIDDLE C

Purse or pucker the lips to play hole 4 only. It is a BLOW **C** note.

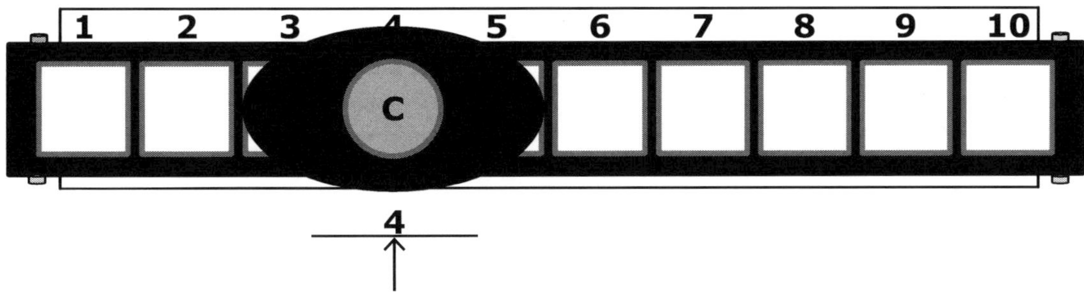

Use the lips to seal the adjacent holes and escaping air over or under the mouthpiece so that only '***one***' **single hole** receives the air in or out of the harmonica. No air leakage.

Middle C appears on a 'short' added line (ledger line) below the staff

Example 1: The C Note

Practice counting evenly; use four (4) counts per measure with a steady rhythm.

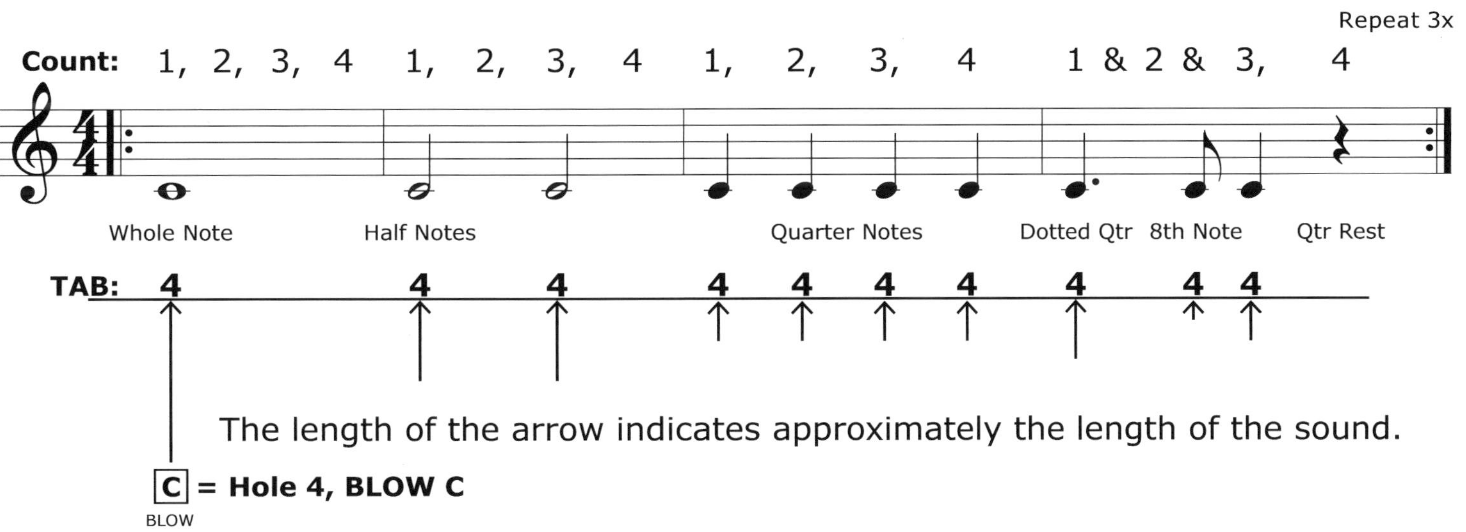

TABLATURE REMINDER:

1. **UPPER CASE** letters are **BLOW** tones
2. lower case letters are draw tones
3. **LARGE numbers** are **BLOW** tones
4. small numbers are draw tones

CHAPTER 1

THE MIDDLE HOLES

Exhale = ↑ Inhale = ↓

Letters: C, d - E, f - G, a
Holes: 4, 5, 6

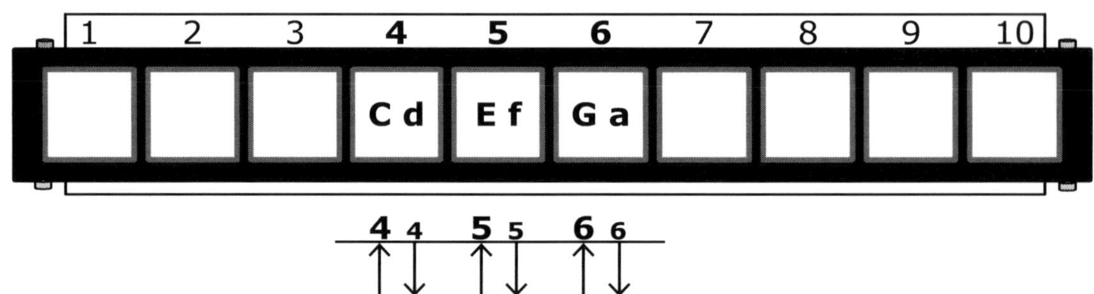

Example 2:

Holes: 4, 5, 6

Exhale = ↑ Inhale = ↓

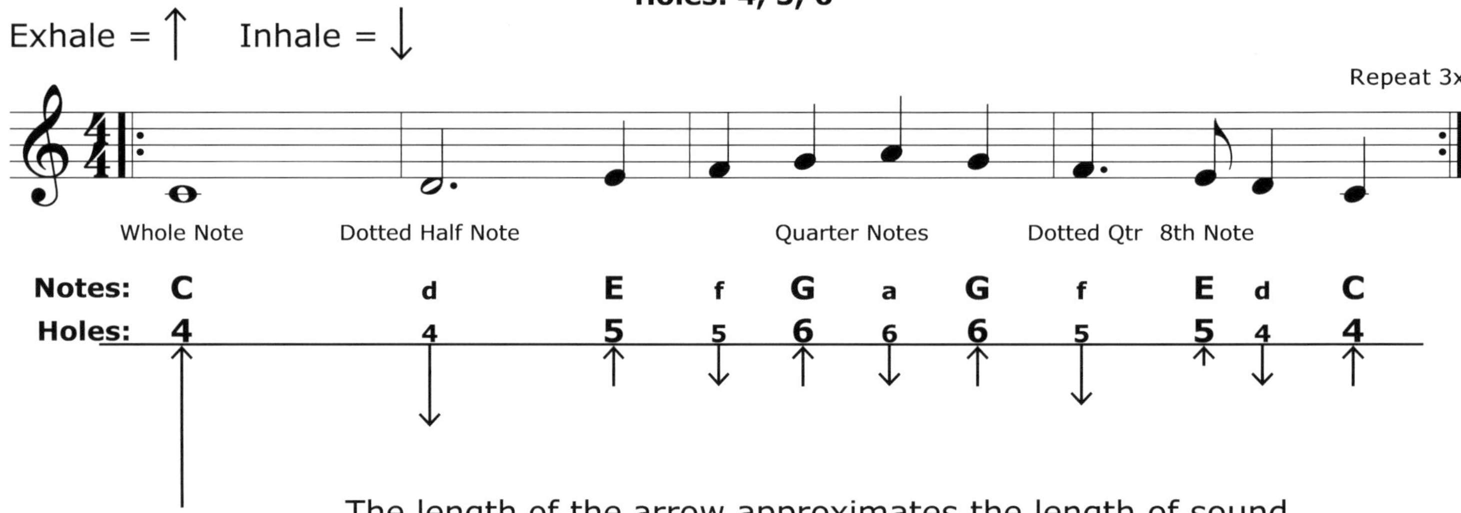

The length of the arrow approximates the length of sound.

TIPS ON PERFORMANCE

Play each set of four (4) measures, called a phrase, until the complete song is accomplished and memorized. Music should be performed without looking at the song.
Also, if a short passage seems difficult, play it several times before starting over.

The following tunes/songs include these single tones:
Holes: 4, 5, 6

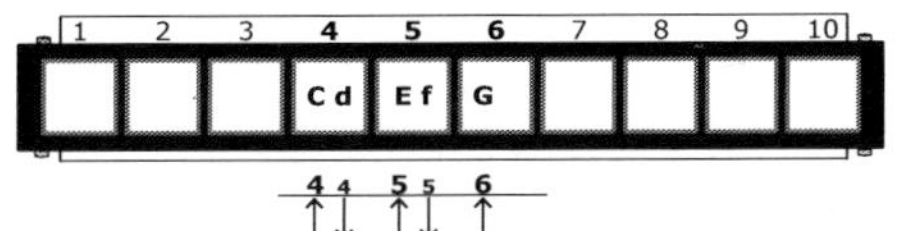

Some Folks Do

Blow = ↑ Draw = ↓

Large Number = BLOW
small number = draw

Folk Music

Traditional

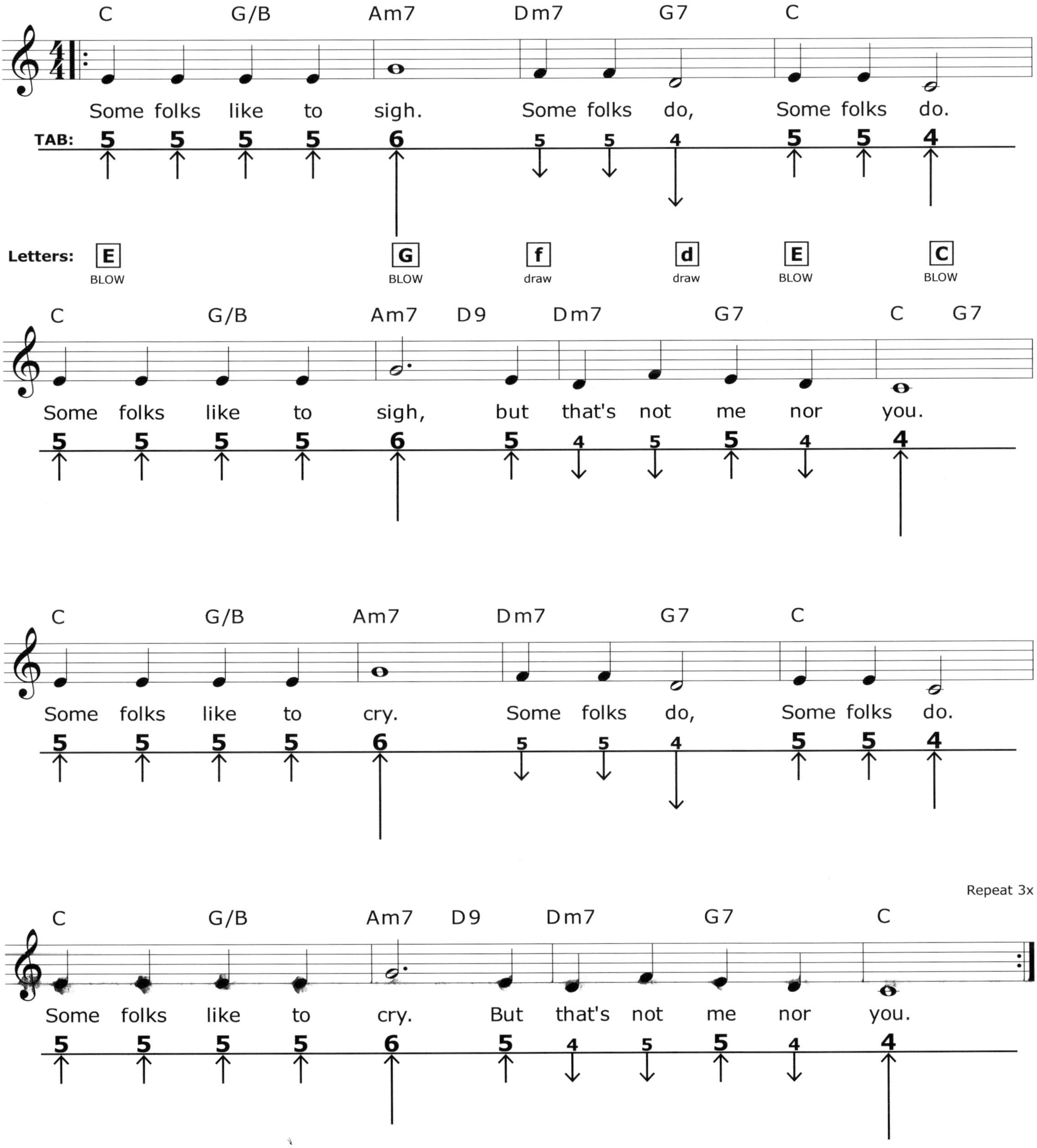

C G/B Am7 Dm7 G7 C

Some folks like to sigh. Some folks do, Some folks do.

TAB: 5↑ 5↑ 5↑ 5↑ 6↑ 5↓ 5↓ 4↓ 5↑ 5↑ 4↑

Letters: E BLOW, G BLOW, f draw, d draw, E BLOW, C BLOW

C G/B Am7 D9 Dm7 G7 C G7

Some folks like to sigh, but that's not me nor you.

5↑ 5↑ 5↑ 5↑ 6↑ 5↑ 4↓ 5↓ 5↑ 4↓ 4↑

C G/B Am7 Dm7 G7 C

Some folks like to cry. Some folks do, Some folks do.

5↑ 5↑ 5↑ 5↑ 6↑ 5↓ 5↓ 4↓ 5↑ 5↑ 4↑

Repeat 3x

C G/B Am7 D9 Dm7 G7 C

Some folks like to cry. But that's not me nor you.

5↑ 5↑ 5↑ 5↑ 6↑ 5↑ 4↓ 5↓ 5↑ 4↓ 4↑

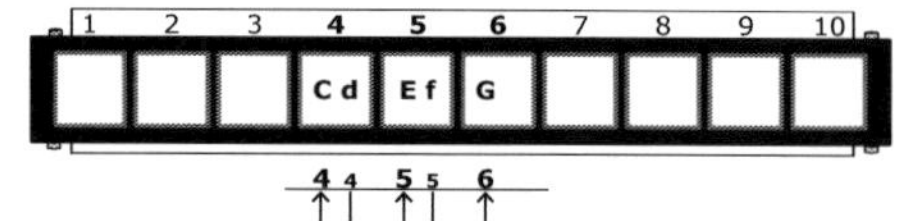

Boil the Cabbage Down

Blow = ↑ Draw = ↓

Large Number = BLOW
small number = draw

Folk Music

Traditional

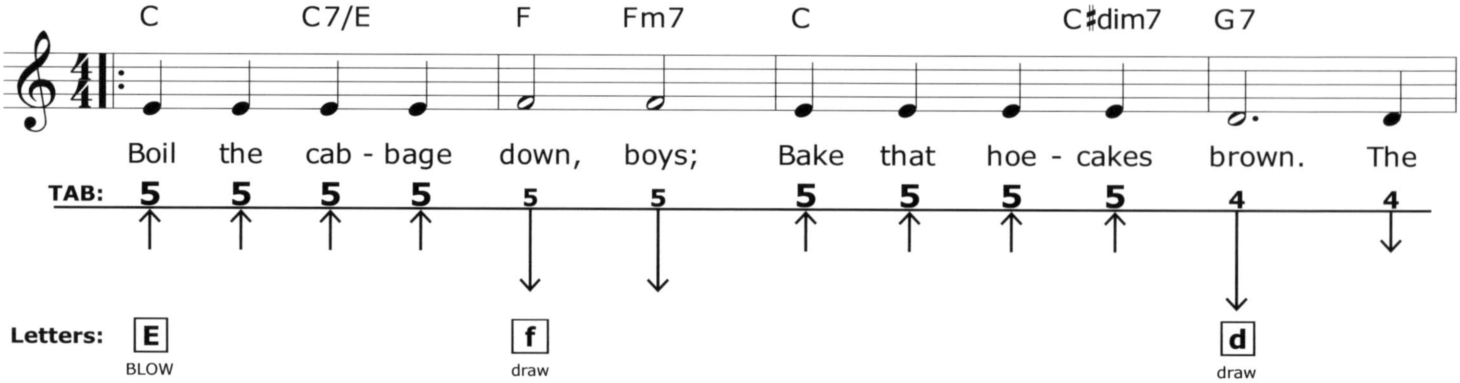

C C7/E F Fm7 C C♯dim7 G7

Boil the cab - bage down, boys; Bake that hoe - cakes brown. The

TAB: 5↑ 5↑ 5↑ 5↑ 5↓ 5↓ 5↑ 5↑ 5↑ 5↑ 4↓ 4↓

Letters: E BLOW, f draw, d draw

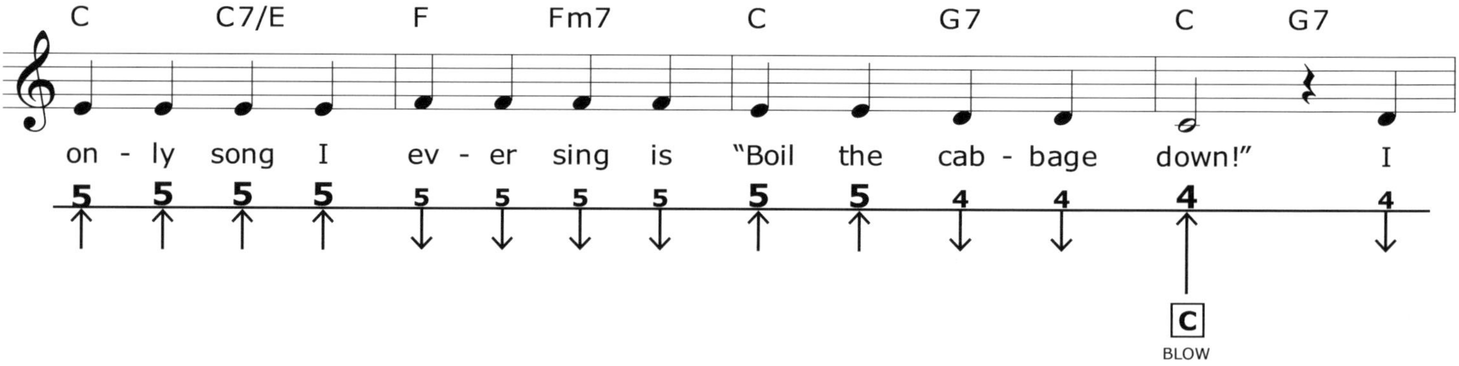

C C7/E F Fm7 C G7 C G7

on - ly song I ev - er sing is "Boil the cab - bage down!" I

5↑ 5↑ 5↑ 5↑ 5↓ 5↓ 5↓ 5↓ 5↑ 5↑ 4↓ 4↓ 4↑ 4↓

C BLOW

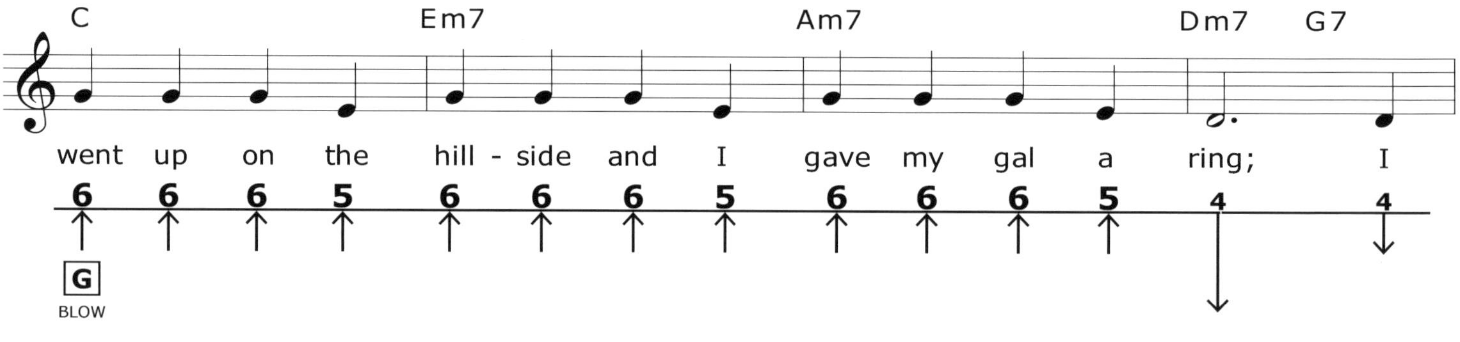

C Em7 Am7 Dm7 G7

went up on the hill - side and I gave my gal a ring; I

6↑ 6↑ 6↑ 5↑ 6↑ 6↑ 6↑ 5↑ 6↑ 6↑ 6↑ 5↑ 4↓ 4↓

G BLOW

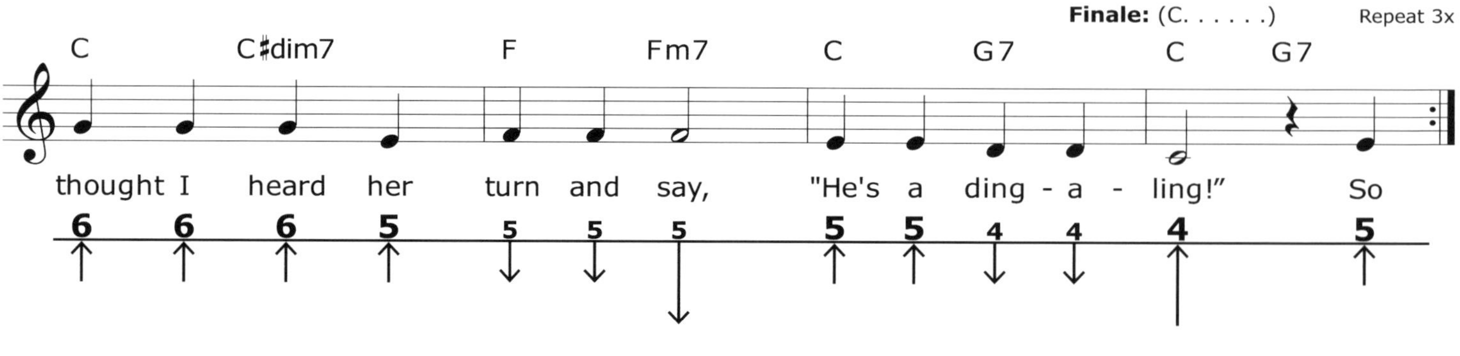

Finale: (C. . . . . .) Repeat 3x

C C♯dim7 F Fm7 C G7 C G7

thought I heard her turn and say, "He's a ding - a - ling!" So

6↑ 6↑ 6↑ 5↑ 5↓ 5↓ 5↓ 5↑ 5↑ 4↓ 4↓ 4↑ 5↑

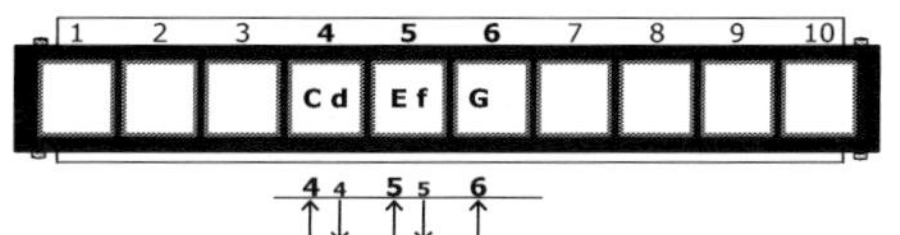

Oh, When the Saints

(Go Marching in)

Large Number = BLOW
small number = draw

Folk Music

Spiritual

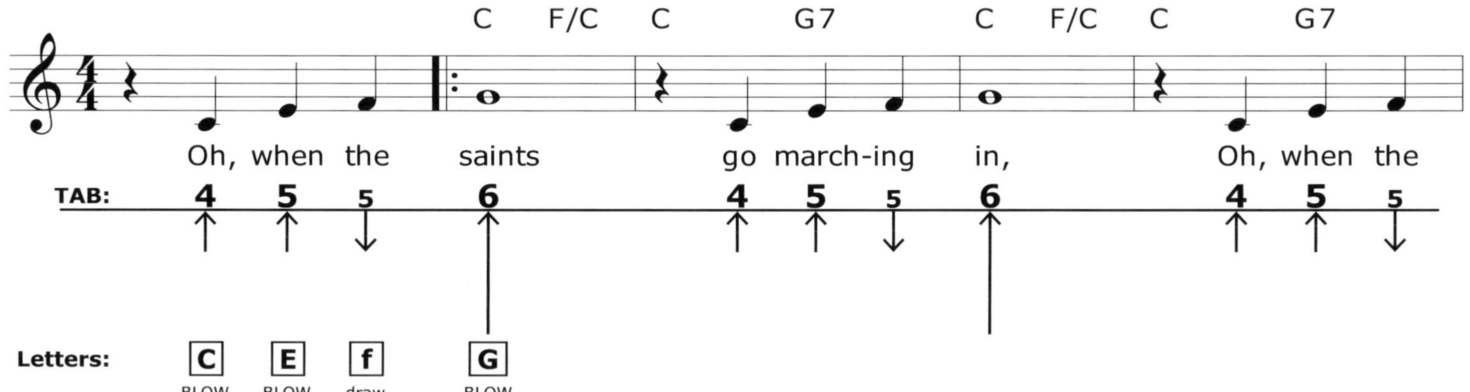

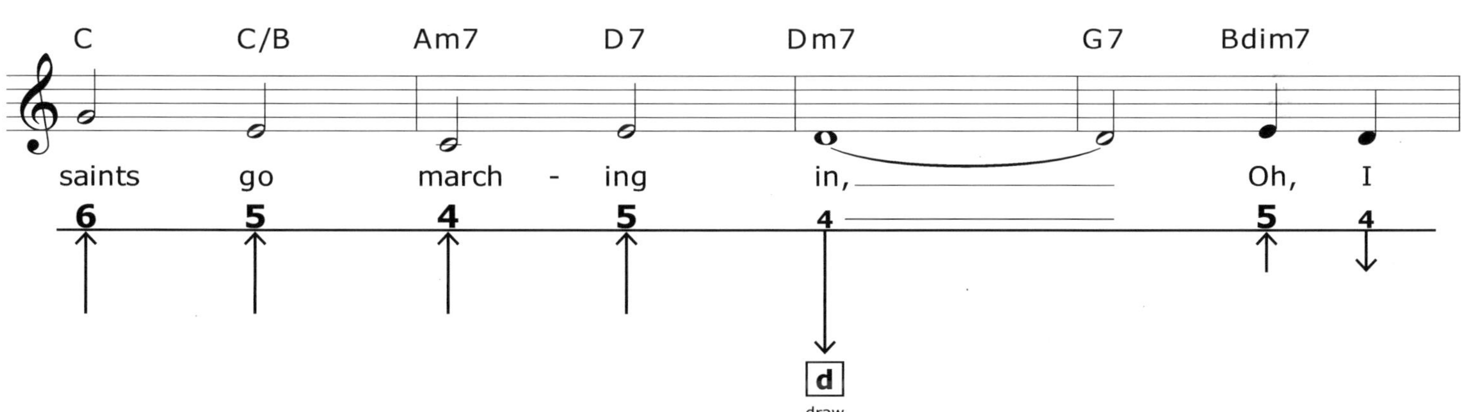

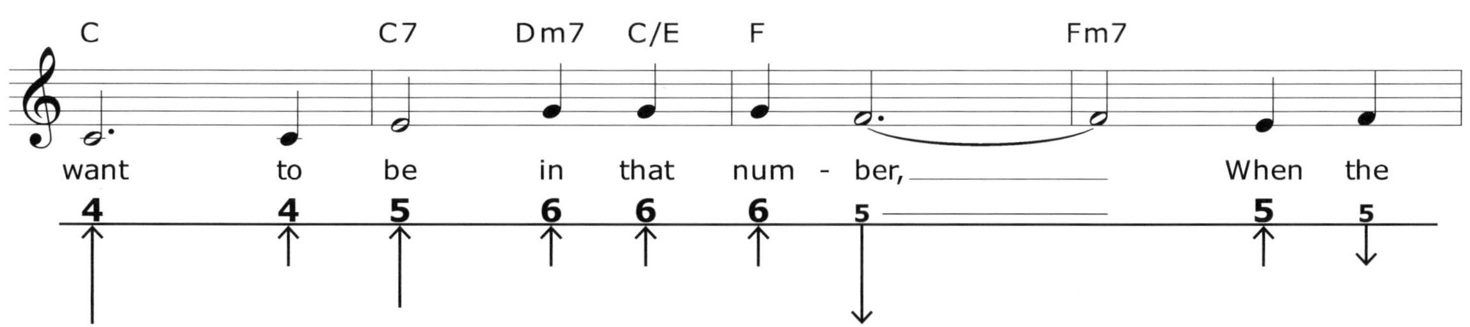

Repeat 3x

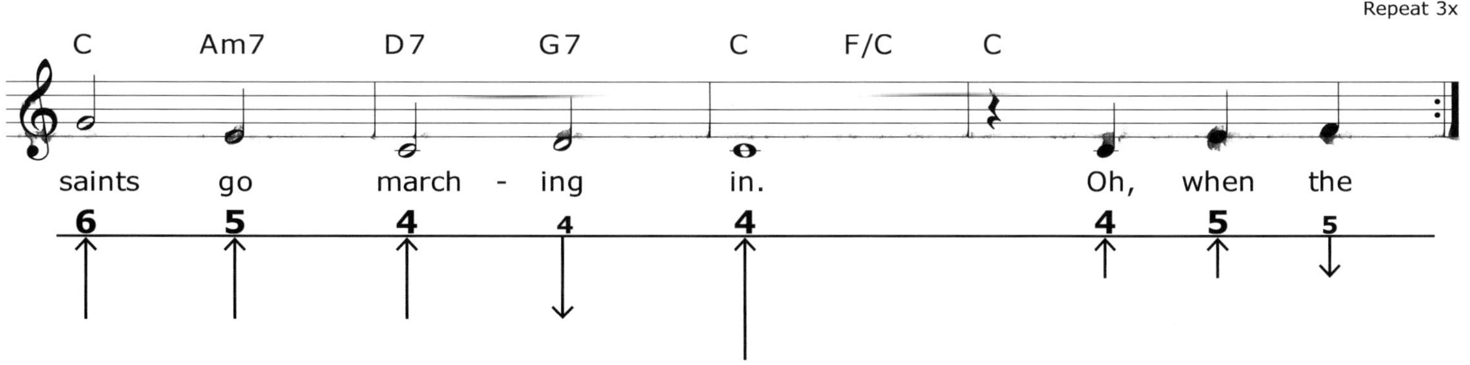

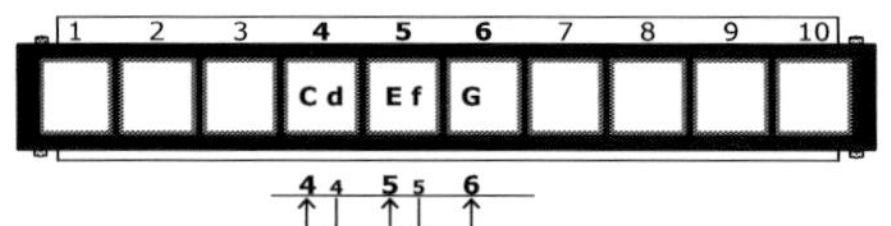

Jingle Bells

Large Number = BLOW
small number = draw

Christmas

J. Pierpoint

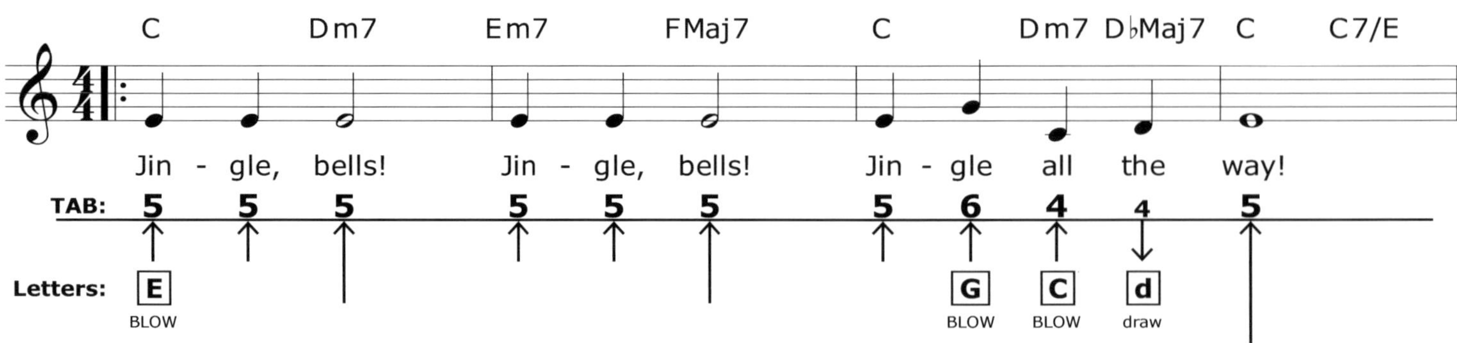

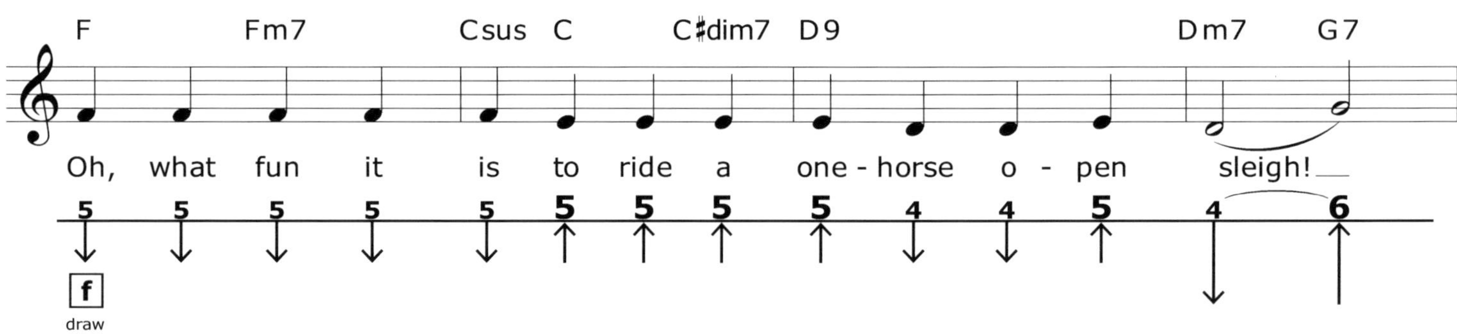

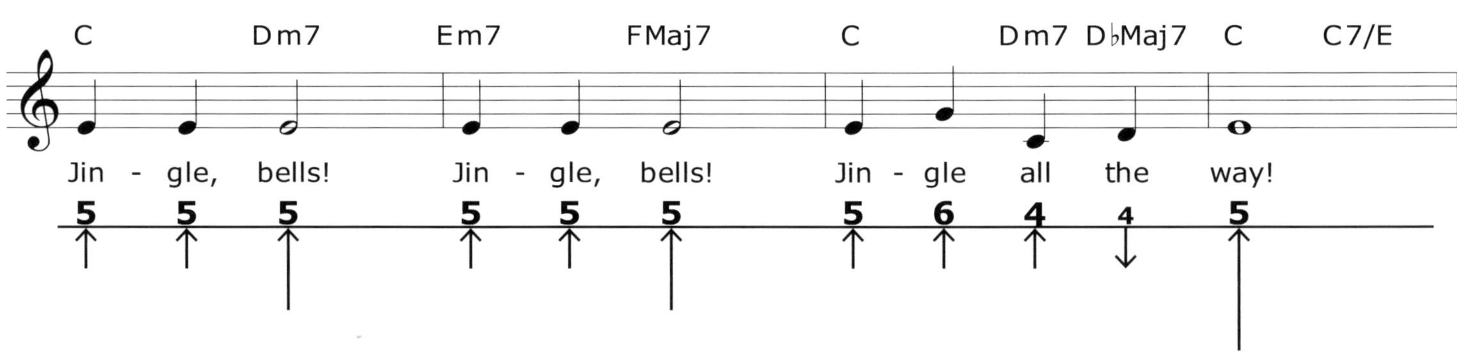

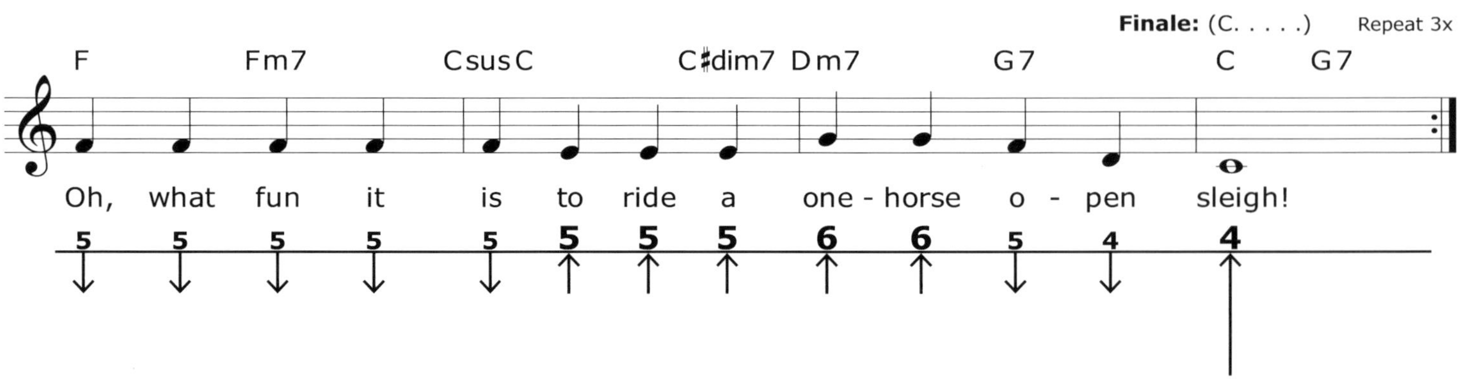

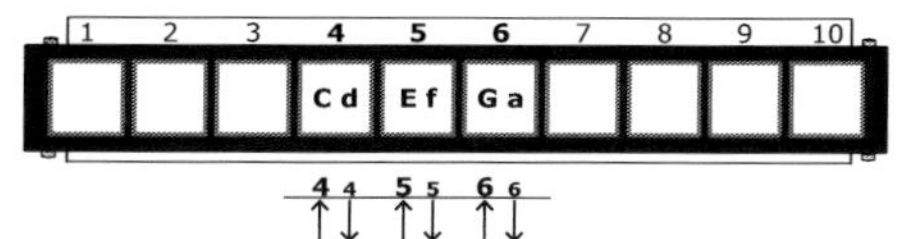

For He's a Jolly Good Fellow

Blow = ↑ Draw = ↓

Large Number = BLOW
small number = draw

Only **3** Counts to a measure!

Folk Traditional

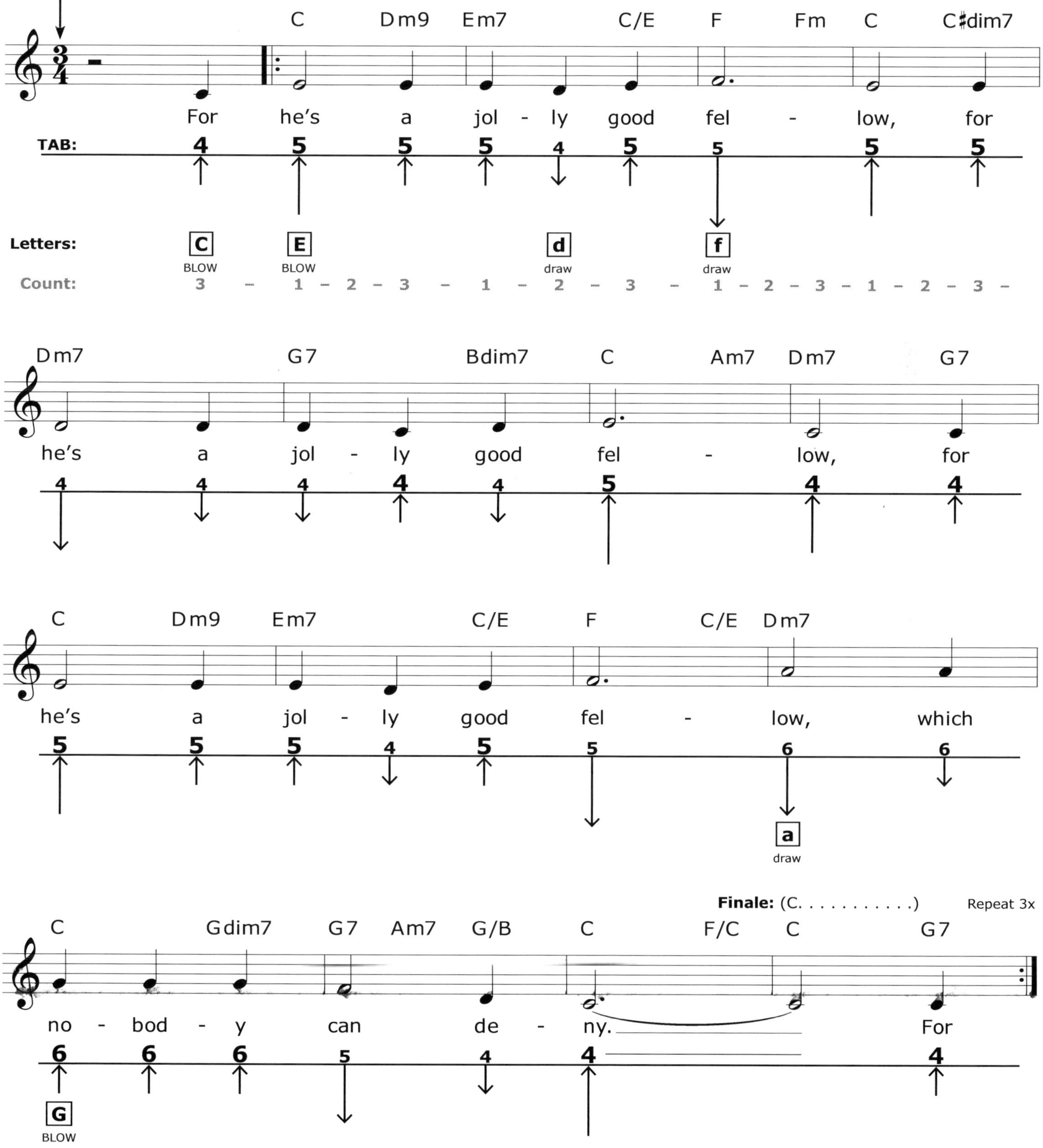

C Dm9 Em7 C/E F Fm C C♯dim7

For he's a jol - ly good fel - low, for

TAB: 4↑ 5↑ 5↑ 5↑ 4↓ 5↑ 5↓ 5↑ 5↑

Letters: C BLOW, E BLOW, d draw, f draw

Count: 3 – 1 – 2 – 3 – 1 – 2 – 3 – 1 – 2 – 3 – 1 – 2 – 3 –

Dm7 G7 Bdim7 C Am7 Dm7 G7

he's a jol - ly good fel - low, for

4↓ 4↓ 4↓ 4↑ 4↓ 5↑ 4↑ 4↑

C Dm9 Em7 C/E F C/E Dm7

he's a jol - ly good fel - low, which

5↑ 5↑ 5↑ 4↓ 5↑ 5↓ 6↓ 6↓

a draw

Finale: (C. . . . .) Repeat 3x

C Gdim7 G7 Am7 G/B C F/C C G7

no - bod - y can de - ny. For

6↑ 6↑ 6↑ 5↓ 4↓ 4↑ 4↑

G BLOW

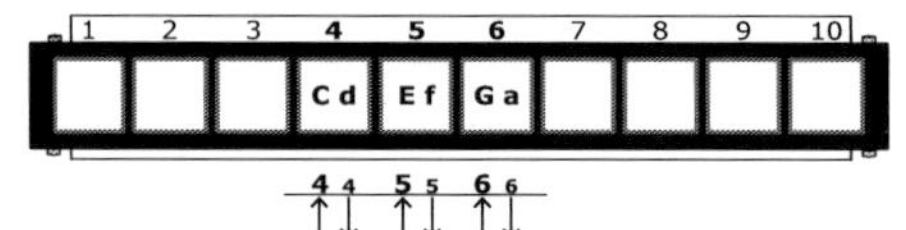

Kum Ba Yah

Large Number = BLOW
small number = draw

Folk Music

Spiritual

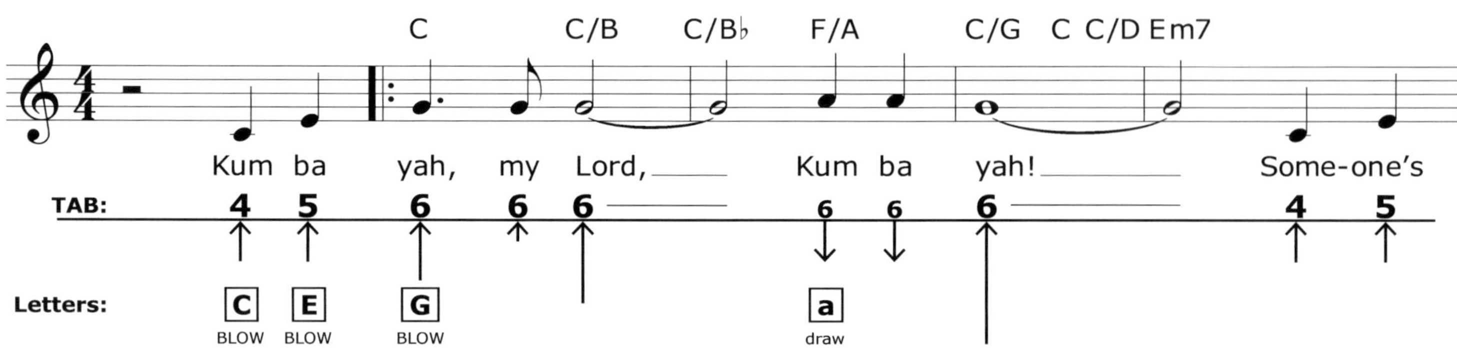

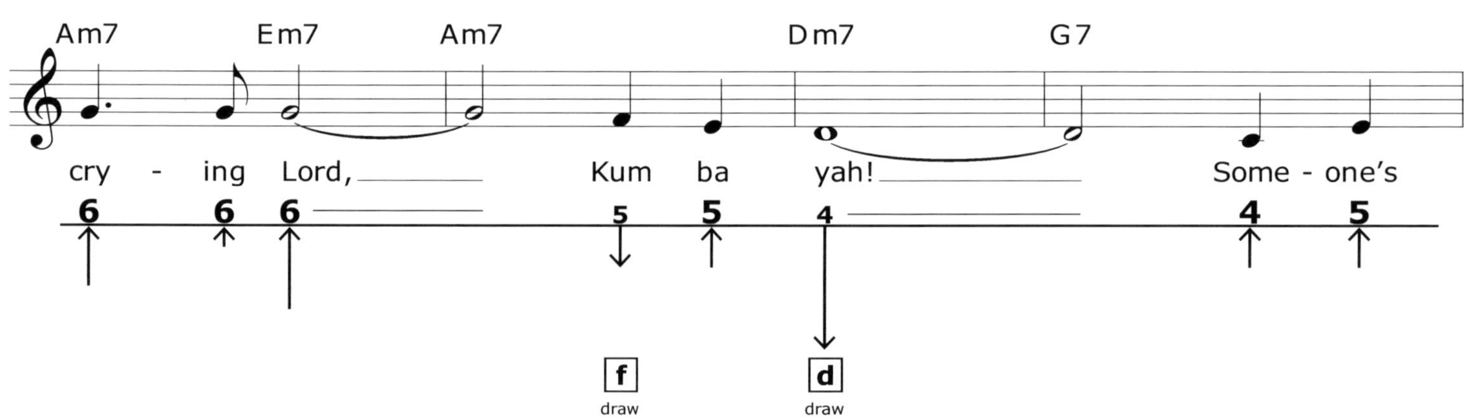

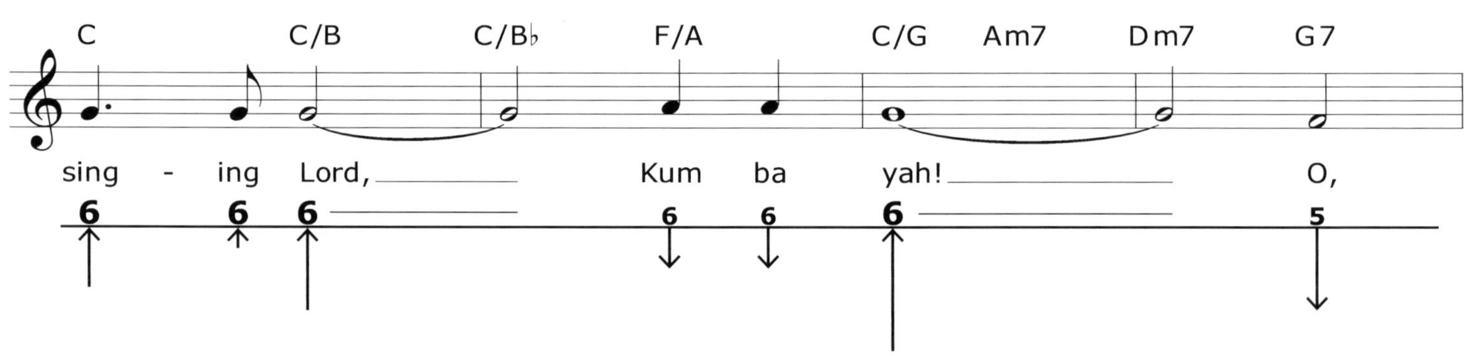

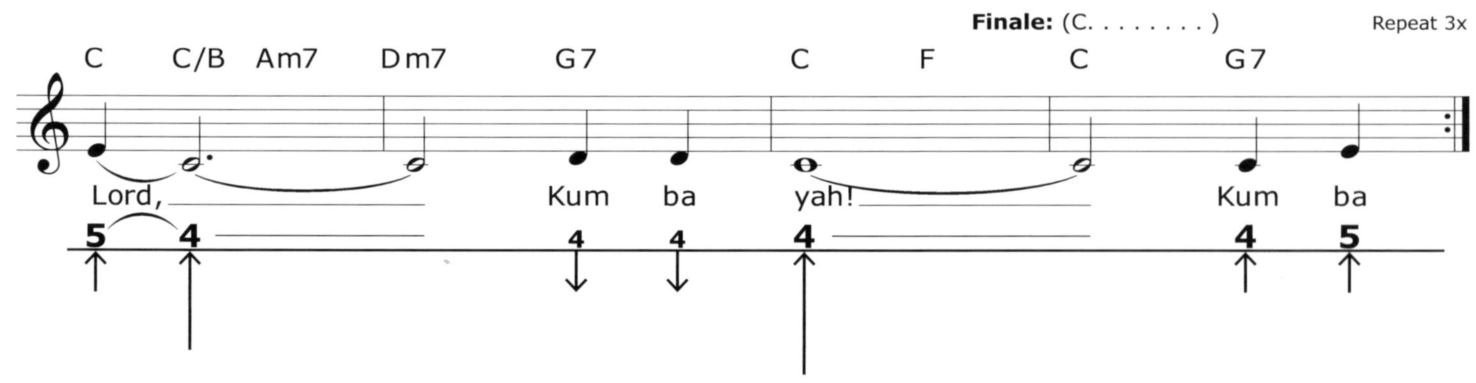

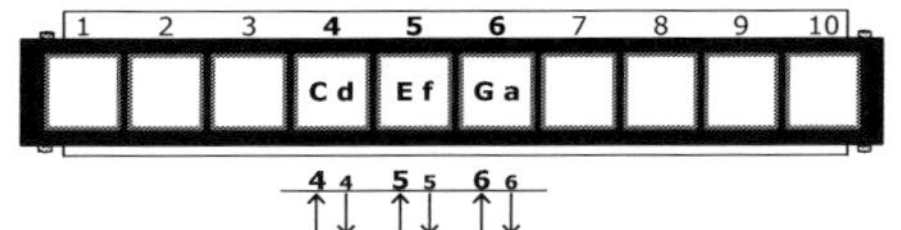

Michael, Row the Boat Ashore

Blow = ↑ Draw = ↓

Large Number = BLOW
small number = draw

Folk Traditional

C | C7 | F | C C/D

Mich - ael, row the boat a - shore, Hal - le - lu - jah, Mich - ael

TAB: 4↑ 5↑ 6↑ 5↑ 6↑ 6↓ 6↑ 5↑ 6↑ 6↓ 6↑ 5↑ 6↑

Letters: C (BLOW) E (BLOW) G (BLOW) a (draw)

Em7 Am7 | Dm9 | G7 | C

row the boat a - shore, Hal - le - lu - jah! Riv - er's

6↑ 5↑ 5↓ 5↑ 4↓ 4↑ 4↓ 5↑ — 4↓ — 4↑ 4↑ 5↑

f (draw) d (draw)

C | C7 | F | C C/D

deep, the riv - er's wide, Hal - le - lu - jah, Riv - er's

6↑ 5↑ 6↑ 6↓ 6↑ 5↑ 6↑ 6↓ 6↑ 5↑ 6↑

Finale: (C. . . . .) Repeat 3x

Em7 Am7 | Dm9 | G7 | C G7

deep, the riv - er's wide. Hal - le - lu - jah! Mich - ael,

6↑ 5↑ 5↓ 5↑ 4↓ 4↑ 4↓ 5↑ — 4↓ — 4↑ 4↑ 5↑

CHAPTER 2

C SCALE

Letters: C, d - E, f - G, a - b, C
Holes: 4 5 6 7

Exhale = ↑ Inhale = ↓ **Holes: 4, 5, 6, 7**

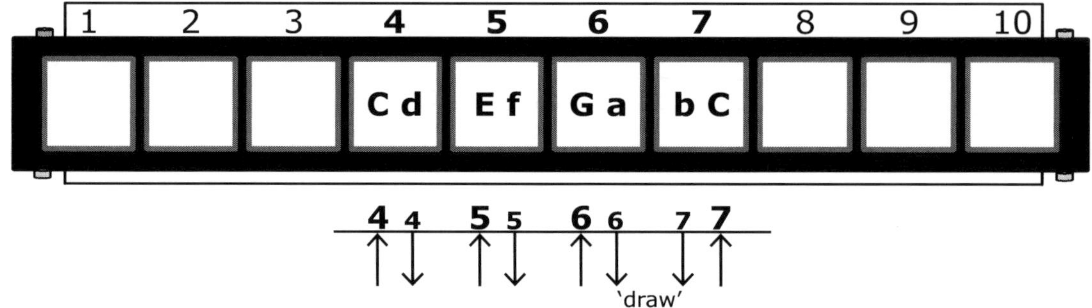

IMPORTANT!

1. After *drawing* the 'a' tone in hole 6, move to hole 7 to *draw* the 'b' tone.
2. Without moving, stay on hole 7, reverse the air flow and *BLOW* High C in hole 7.
3. This allows for a smooth continuation of the scale.

Example 3:

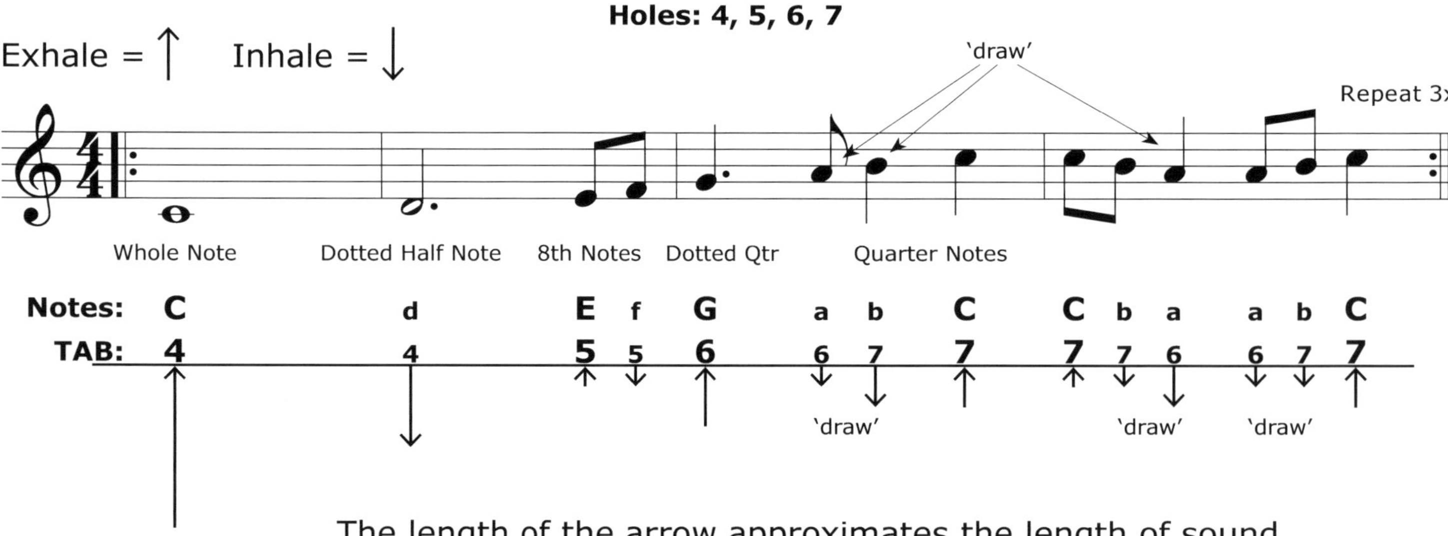

The length of the arrow approximates the length of sound.

The following tunes/songs will use:
Holes: 4, 5, 6, 7

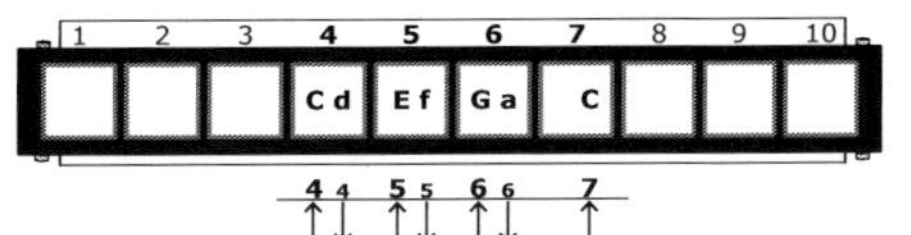

On Top of Old Smokey

Blow = ↑ Draw = ↓

Large Number = BLOW
small number = draw

Waltz
Three (**3**) counts to a measure!

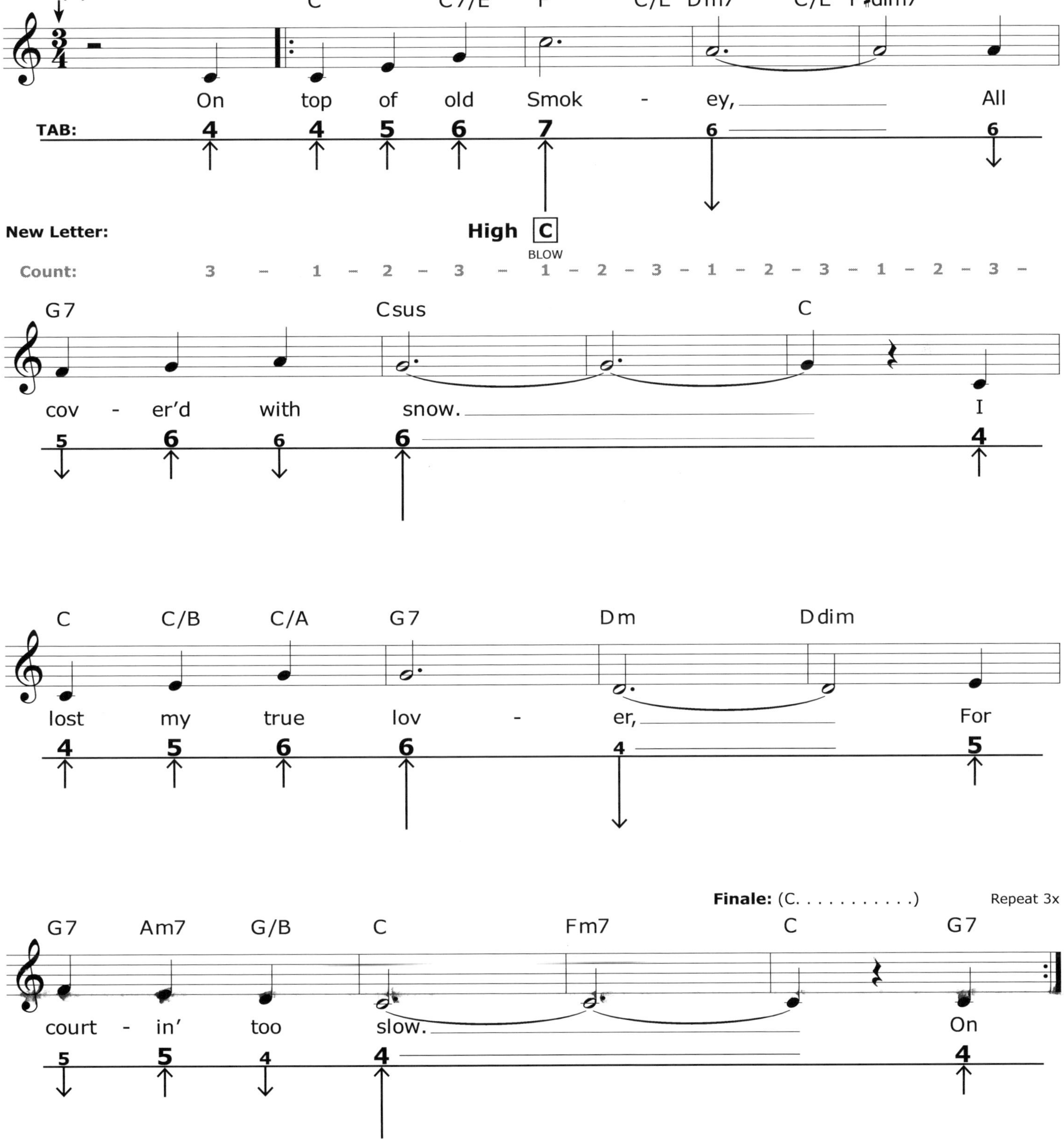

Folk Traditional

C C7/E F C/E Dm7 C/E F♯dim7

On top of old Smok - ey, All

TAB: 4↑ 4↑ 5↑ 6↑ 7↑ 6↓ 6↓

New Letter: **High** C BLOW

Count: 3 – 1 – 2 – 3 – 1 – 2 – 3 – 1 – 2 – 3 – 1 – 2 – 3 –

G7 Csus C

cov - er'd with snow. I

5↓ 6↑ 6↓ 6↑ 4↑

C C/B C/A G7 Dm Ddim

lost my true lov - er, For

4↑ 5↑ 6↑ 6↑ 4↓ 5↑

Finale: (C. . . . .) Repeat 3x

G7 Am7 G/B C Fm7 C G7

court - in' too slow. On

5↓ 5↑ 4↓ 4↑ 4↑

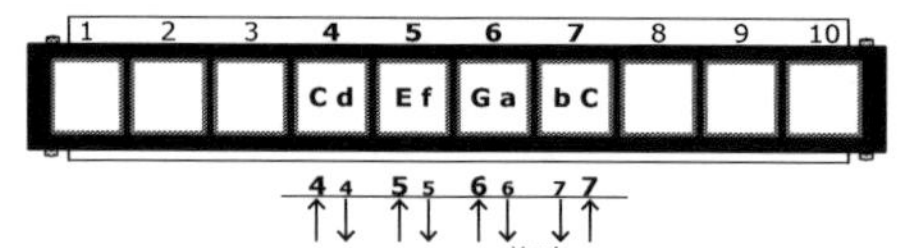

Lullaby and Good Night

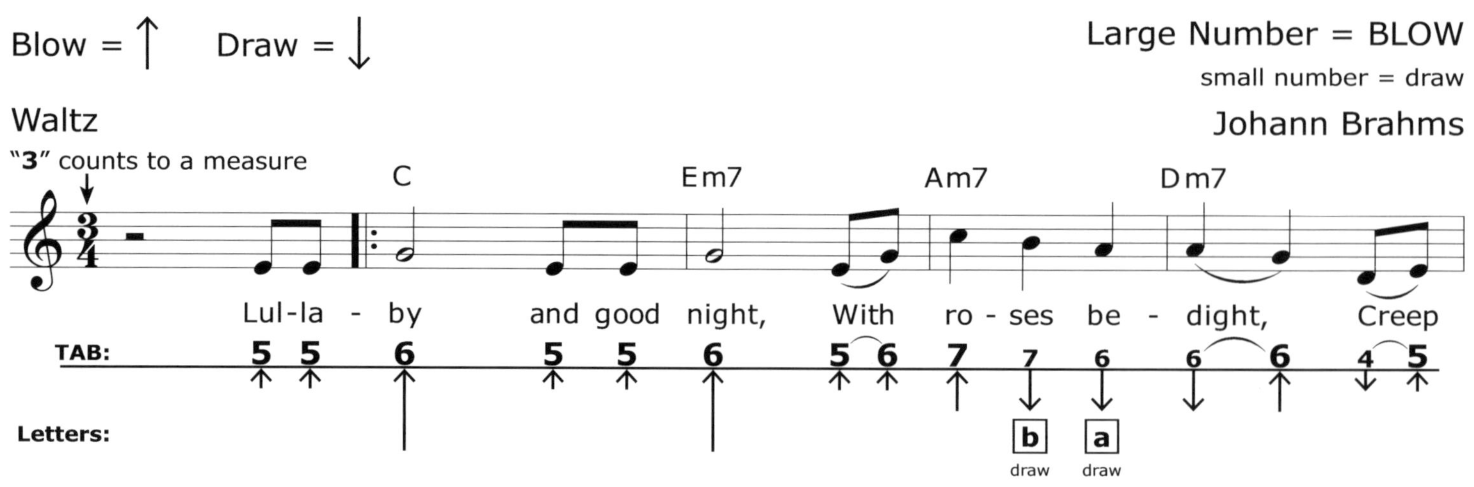

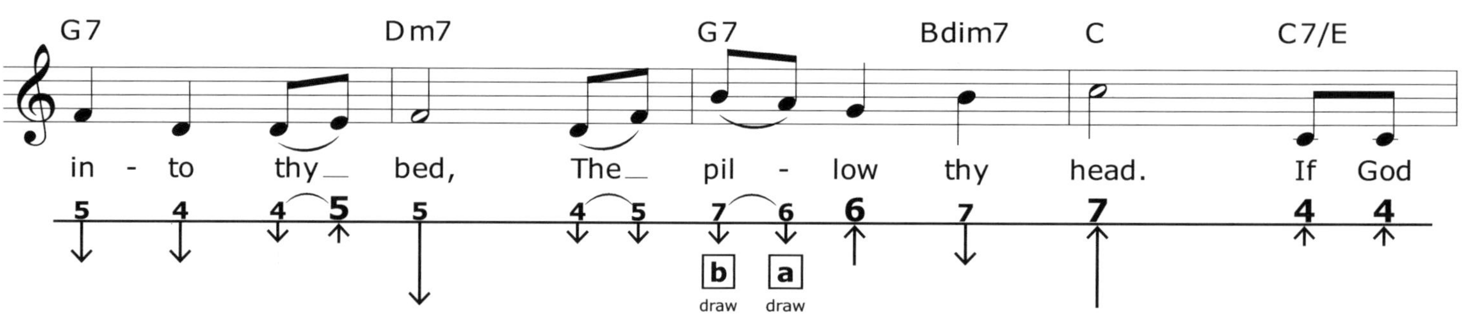

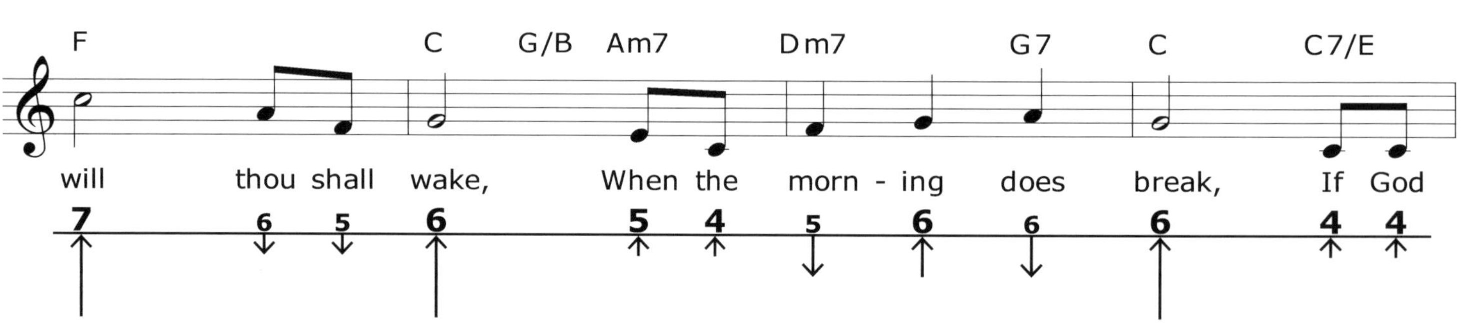

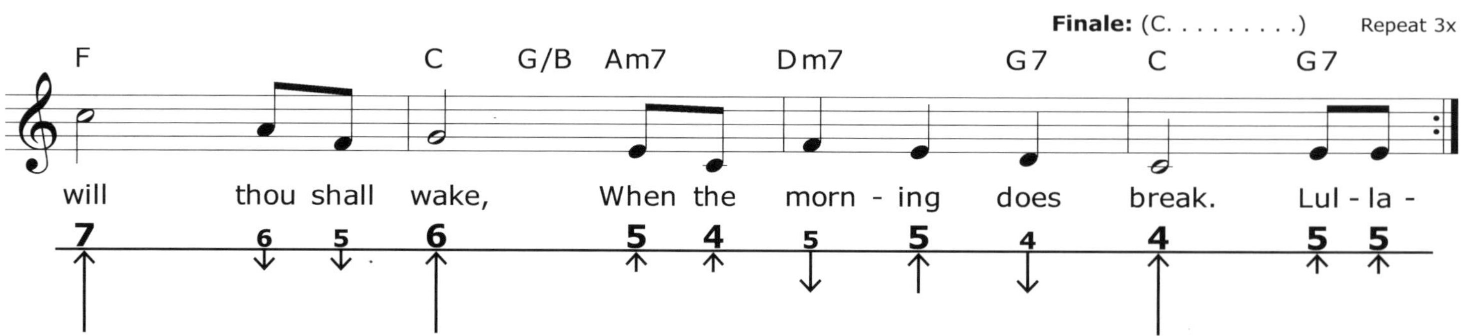

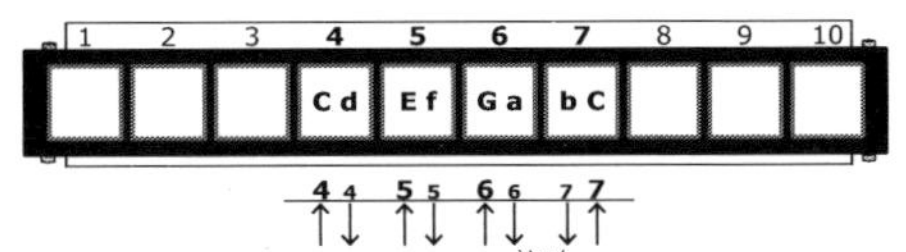

Joy to the World

Blow = ↑ Draw = ↓

Large Number = BLOW
small number = draw

Christmas

George F. Handel

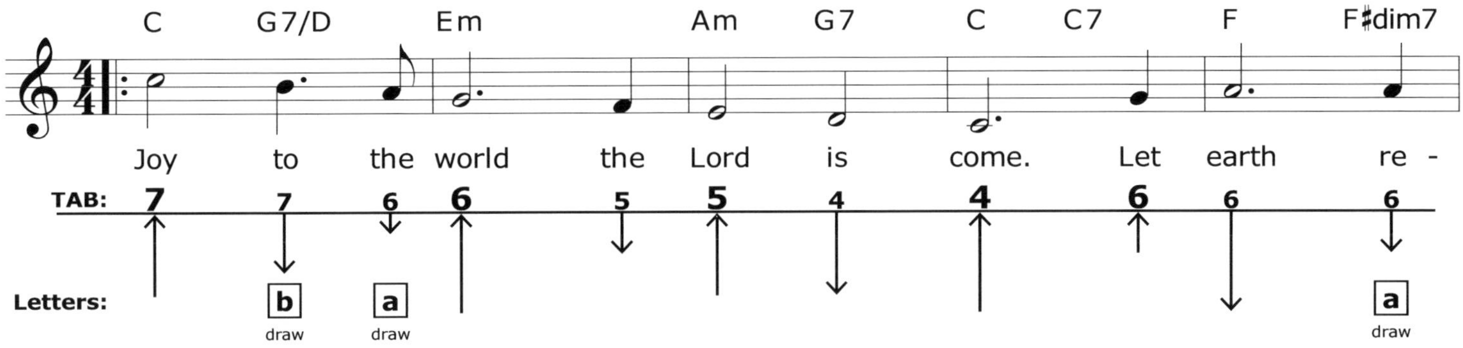

C G7/D Em Am G7 C C7 F F♯dim7

Joy to the world the Lord is come. Let earth re -

TAB: 7↑ 7↓ 6↓ 6↑ 5↓ 5↑ 4↓ 4↑ 6↑ 6↓ 6↓

Letters: b (draw) a (draw) a (draw)

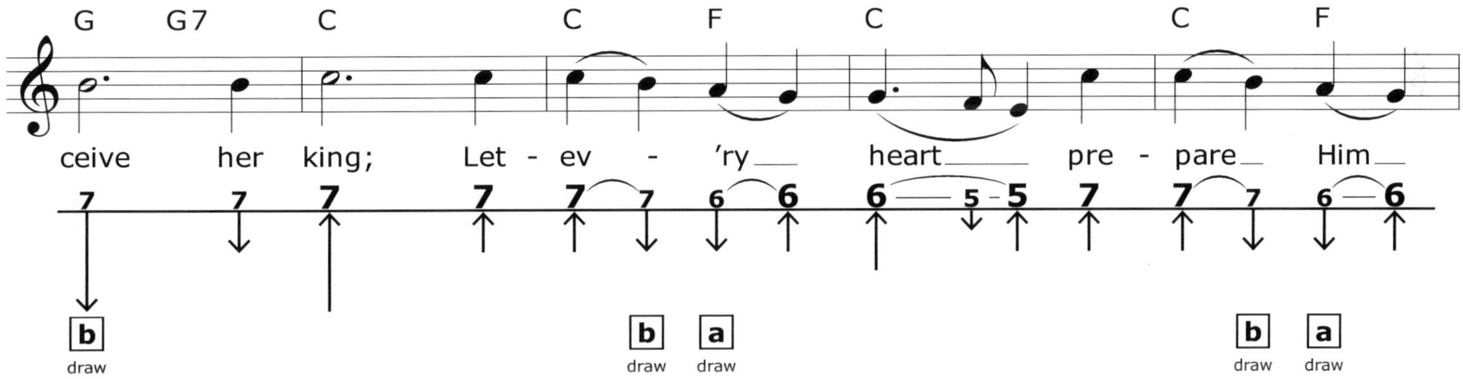

G G7 C C F C C F

ceive her king; Let - ev - 'ry__ heart___ pre - pare_ Him__

7↓ 7↓ 7↑ 7↑ 7↑ 7↓ 6↓ 6↑ 6↑ 5↓ 5↑ 7↑ 7↑ 7↓ 6↓ 6↑

b (draw) b (draw) a (draw) b (draw) a (draw)

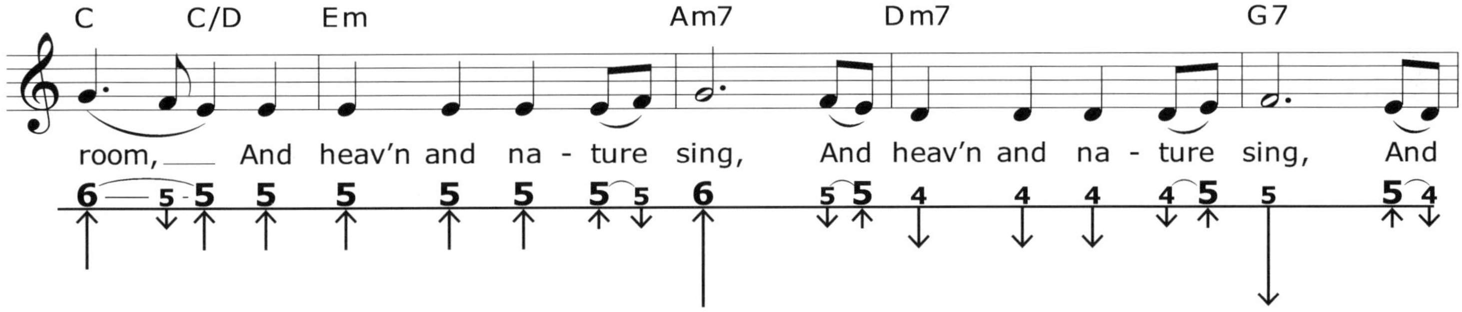

C C/D Em Am7 Dm7 G7

room,__ And heav'n and na - ture sing, And heav'n and na - ture sing, And

6↑ 5↓ 5↑ 5↑ 5↑ 5↑ 5↑ 5↑ 5↓ 6↑ 5↓ 5↑ 4↓ 4↓ 4↓ 4↓ 5↑ 5↓ 5↑ 4↓

Finale: (C. . . . .) Repeat 3x

C F C F F/E Dm7 G7 C F C G7

heav'n and heav'n___ and na - ture sing______

4↑ 7↑ 6↓ 6↑ 5↓ 5↑ 5↓ 5↑ 4↓ 4↑

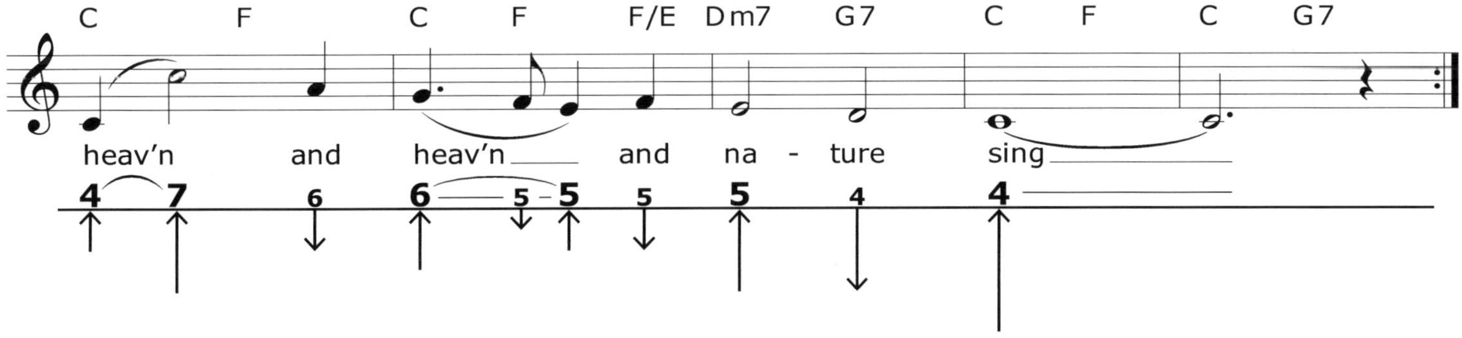

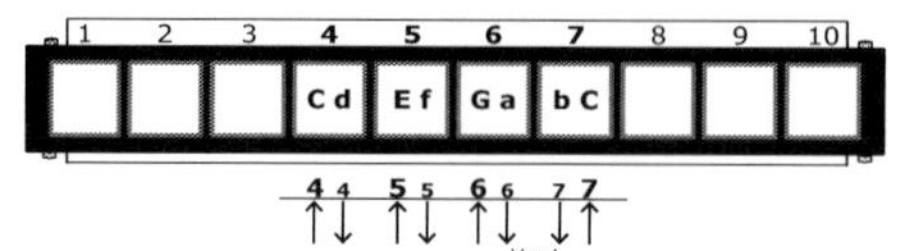

Home, Sweet Home

Blow = ↑ Draw = ↓

Large Number = BLOW
small number = draw

Folk Music

Payne/Bishop

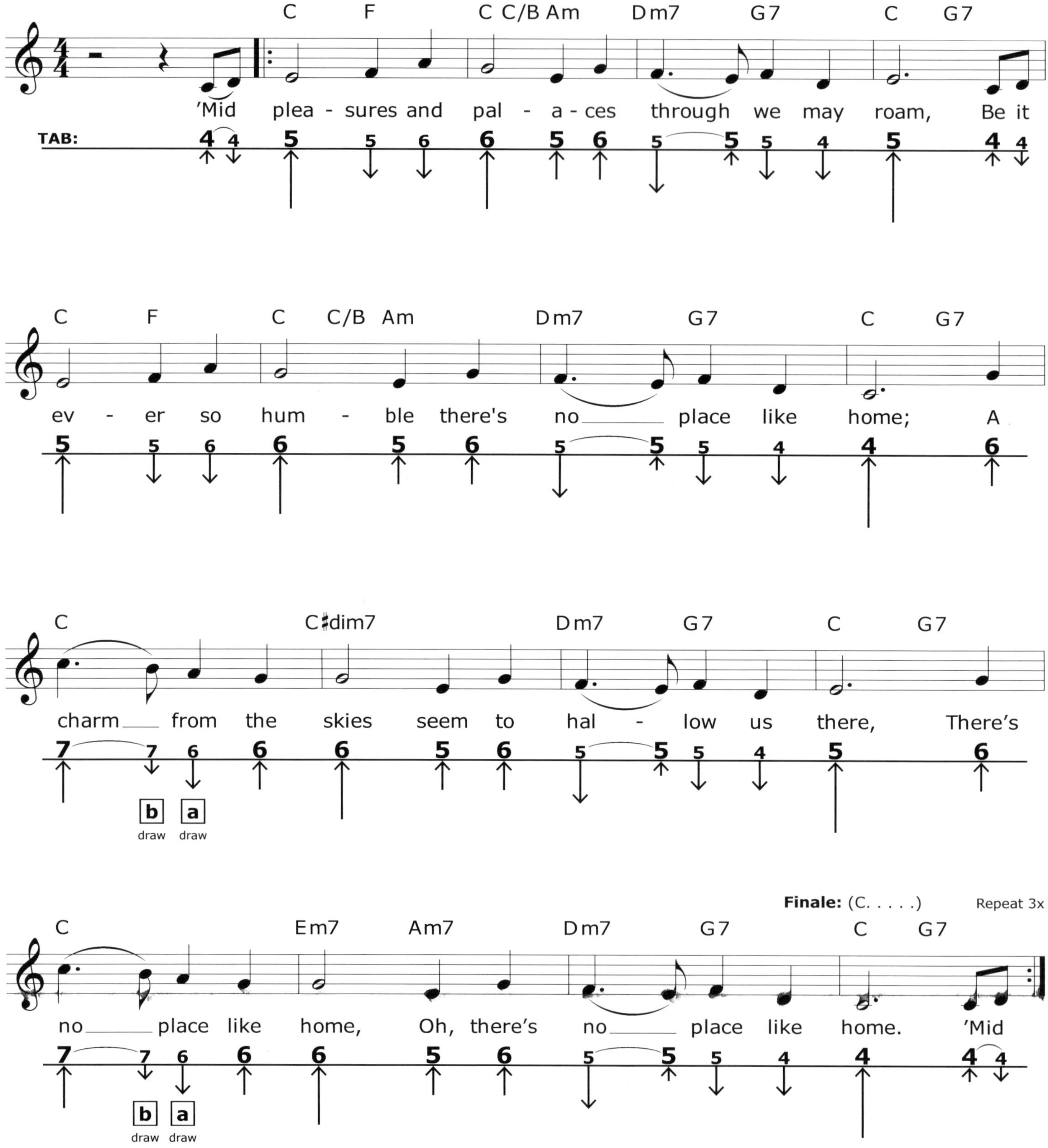

C F C C/B Am Dm7 G7 C G7

'Mid plea - sures and pal - a - ces through we may roam, Be it

TAB: 4 4 5 5 6 6 5 6 5 5 5 4 5 4 4

C F C C/B Am Dm7 G7 C G7

ev - er so hum - ble there's no place like home; A

5 5 6 6 5 6 5 5 5 4 4 6

C C♯dim7 Dm7 G7 C G7

charm from the skies seem to hal - low us there, There's

7 7 6 6 6 5 6 5 5 5 4 5 6

b a
draw draw

Finale: (C. . . . .) Repeat 3x

C Em7 Am7 Dm7 G7 C G7

no place like home, Oh, there's no place like home. 'Mid

7 7 6 6 6 5 6 5 5 5 4 4 4 4

b a
draw draw

CHAPTER 3

LOW END OF THE HARMONICA

Low G and **b** are in between 'Ledger' lines.

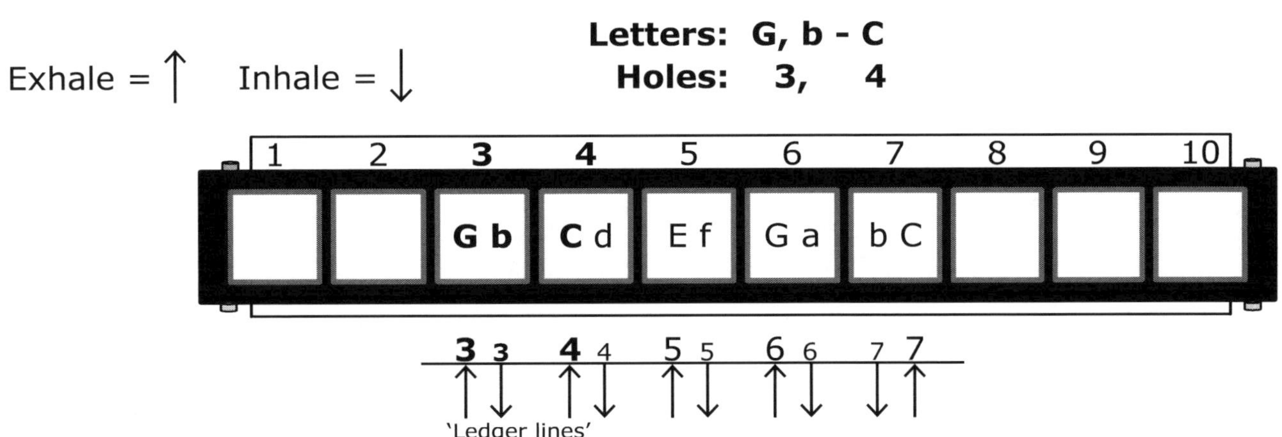

'Ledger' lines are not easy to read. Use the tablature to help find the lower tones.

Example 4:

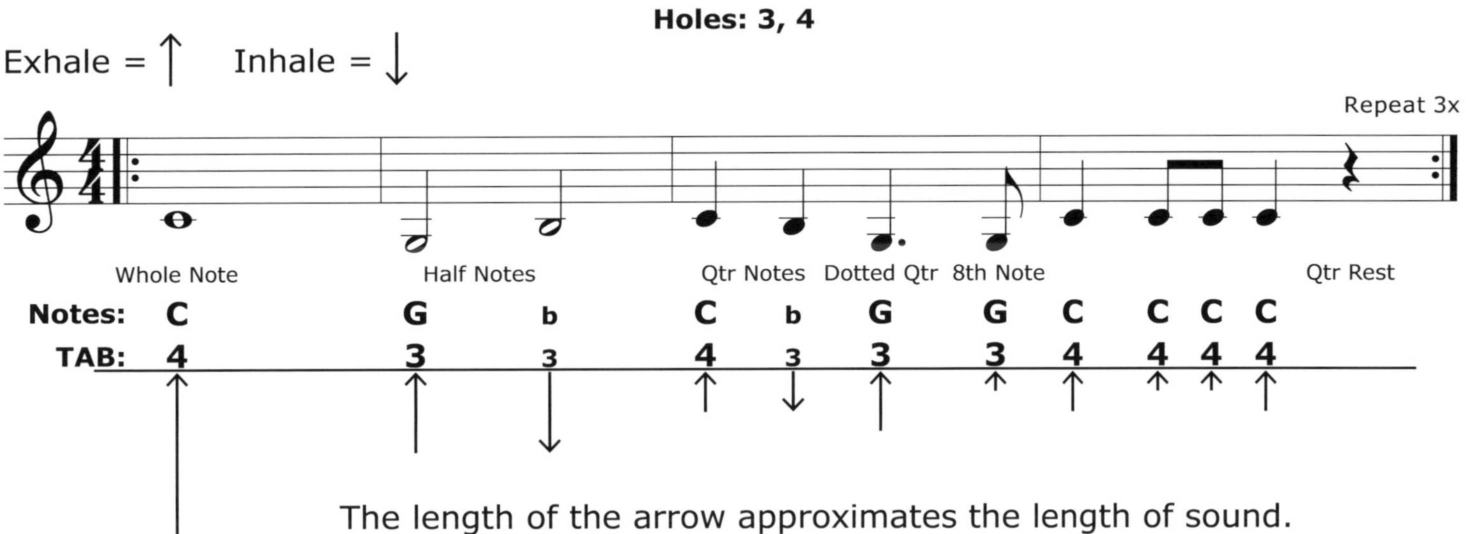

The length of the arrow approximates the length of sound.

PLAYING CHORDS

Holes 1, 2 & 3 are traditionally used for chord playing. Play three holes *at the same time*. The missing notes (f & a) in holes 2 & 3 allow chord playing. Blowing air in holes 1, 2, 3 produces a C chord. Drawing air from holes 1, 2, 3 creates a G chord.

The following tunes/songs add:
Hole: 3

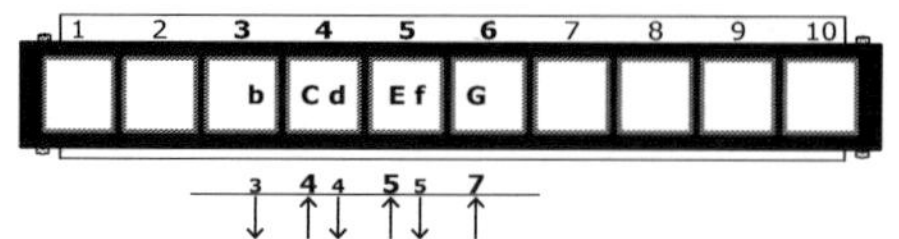

Mary Ann

(Down by the Seashore)

Large Number = BLOW

small number = draw

Folk Ballad

Latin Rhythm

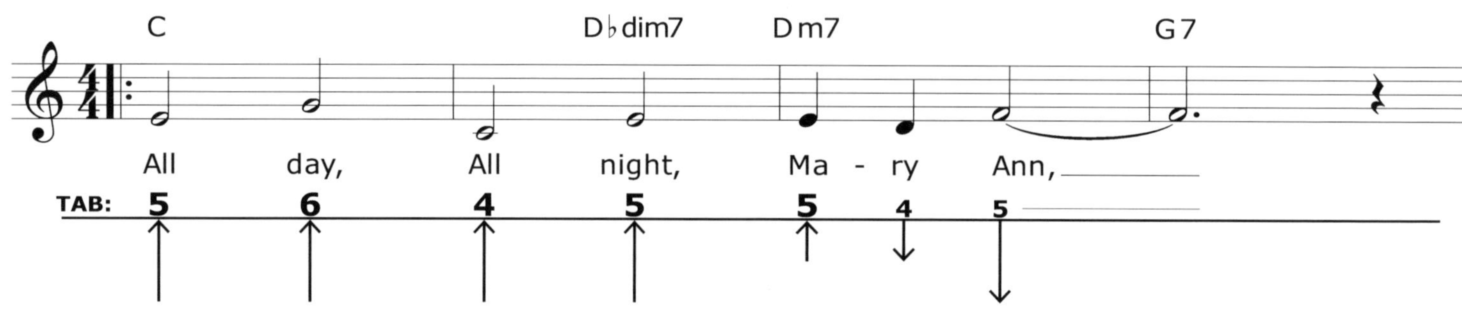

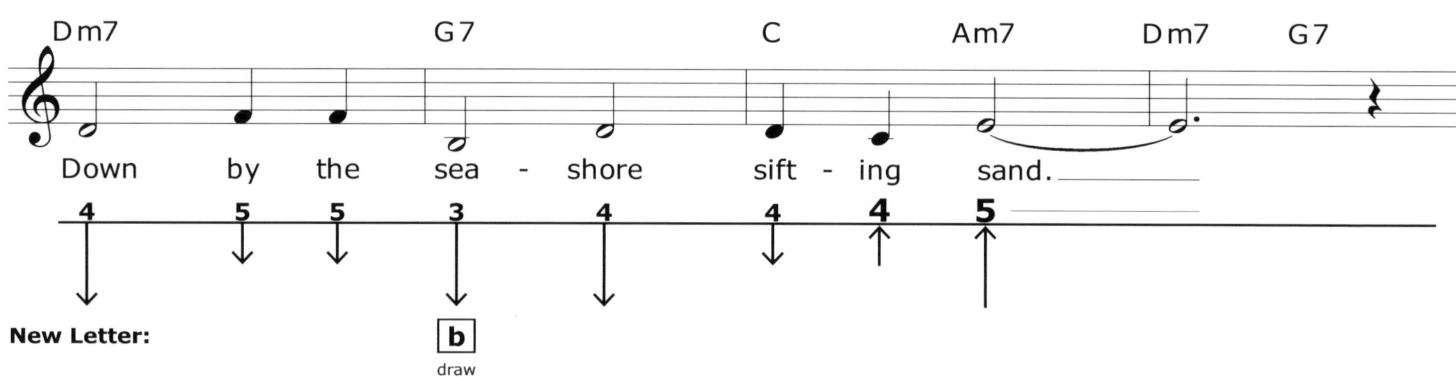

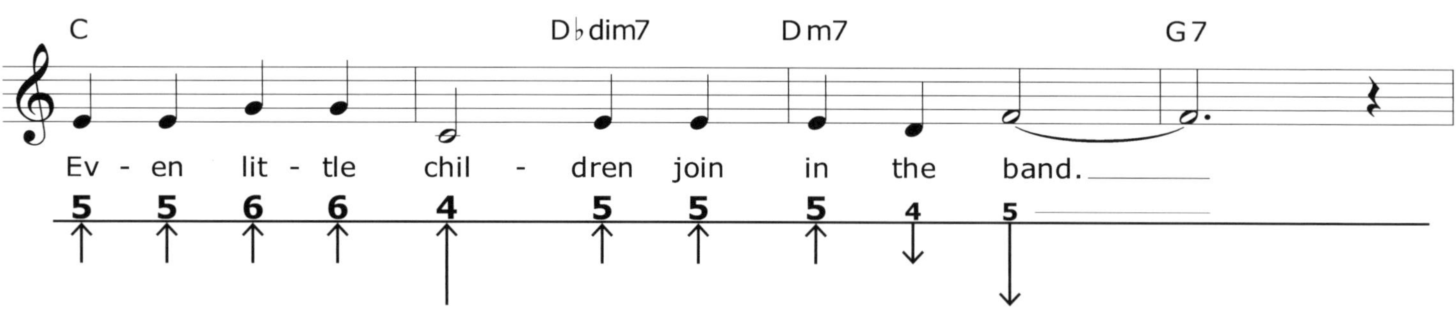

Finale: (C. . . . .) Repeat 3x

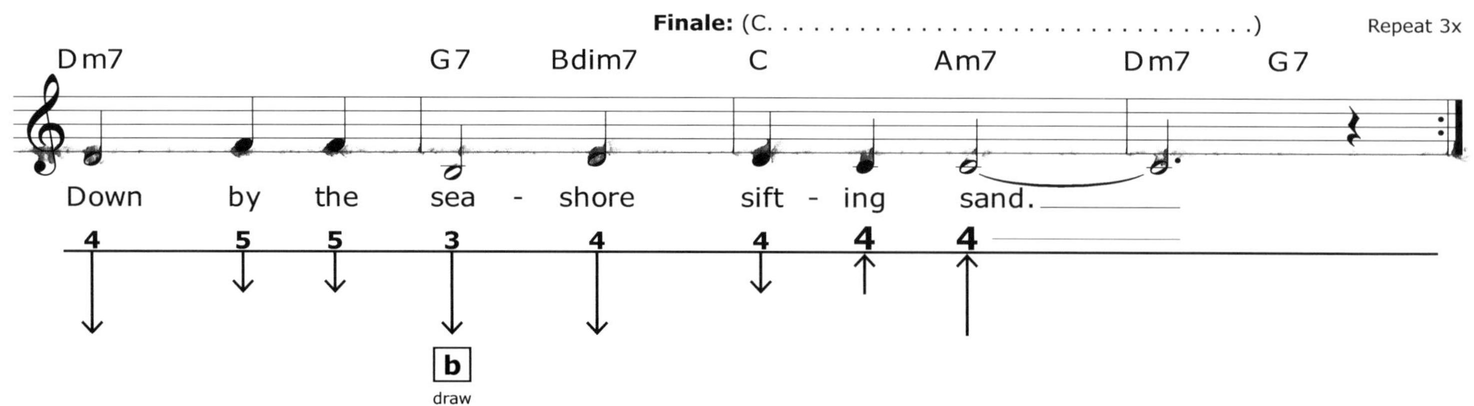

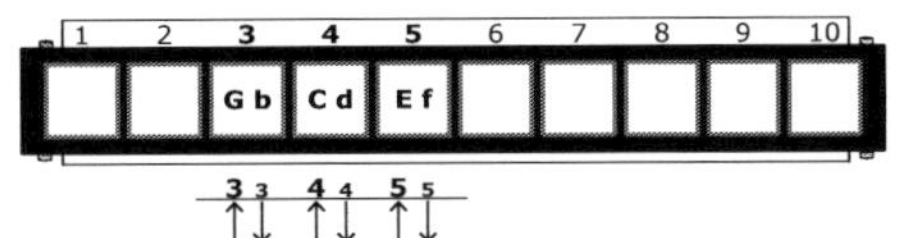

Down in the Valley

Blow = ↑ Draw = ↓

Large Number = BLOW
small number = draw

Folk Music

Traditional

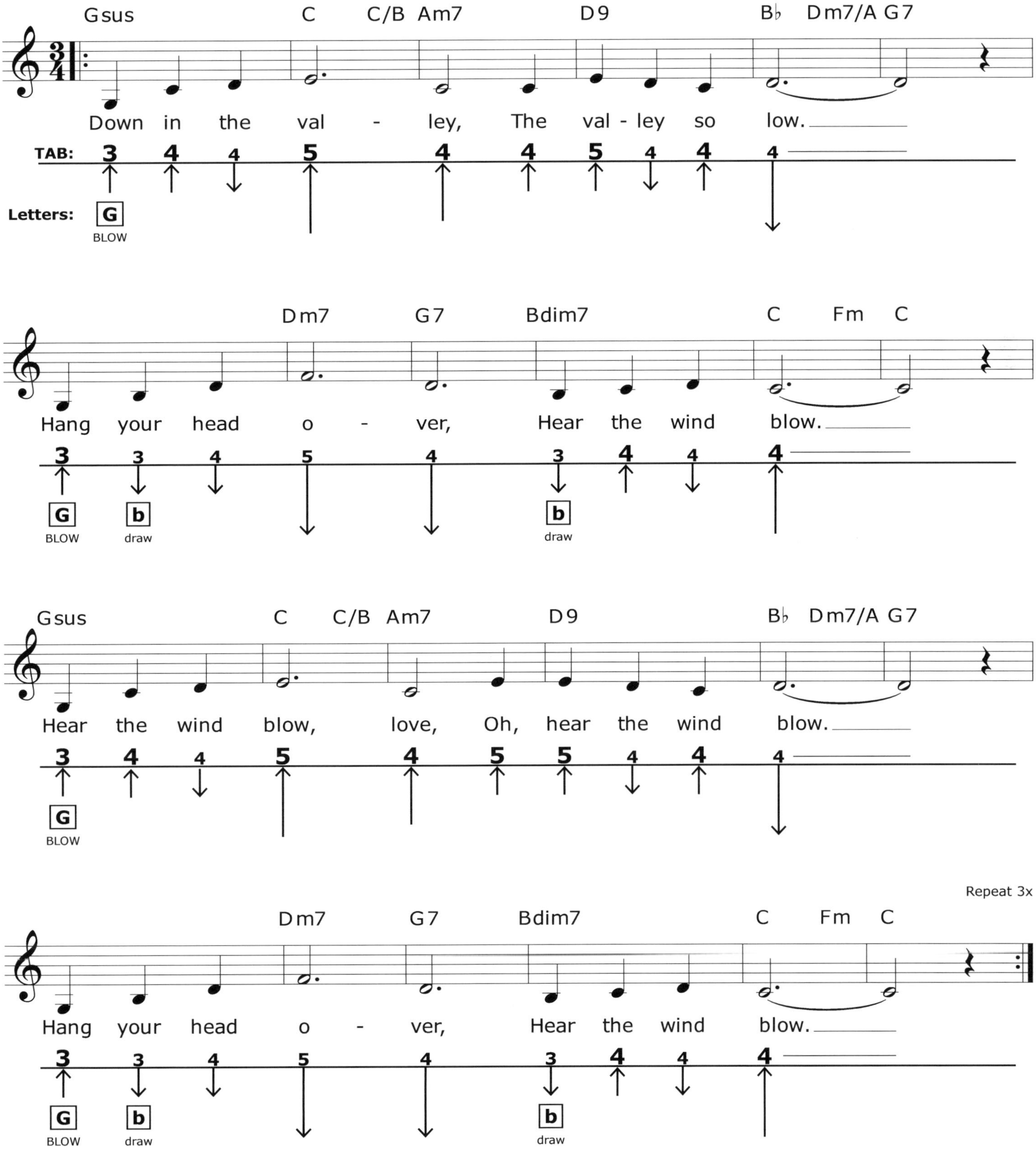

Gsus C C/B Am7 D9 B♭ Dm7/A G7

Down in the val - ley, The val - ley so low. ___

TAB: 3 4 4 5 4 4 5 4 4 4 ___

Letters: G BLOW

Dm7 G7 Bdim7 C Fm C

Hang your head o - ver, Hear the wind blow. ___

3 3 4 5 4 3 4 4 4 ___

G BLOW b draw b draw

Gsus C C/B Am7 D9 B♭ Dm7/A G7

Hear the wind blow, love, Oh, hear the wind blow. ___

3 4 4 5 4 5 5 4 4 4 ___

G BLOW

Repeat 3x

Dm7 G7 Bdim7 C Fm C

Hang your head o - ver, Hear the wind blow. ___

3 3 4 5 4 3 4 4 4 ___

G BLOW b draw b draw

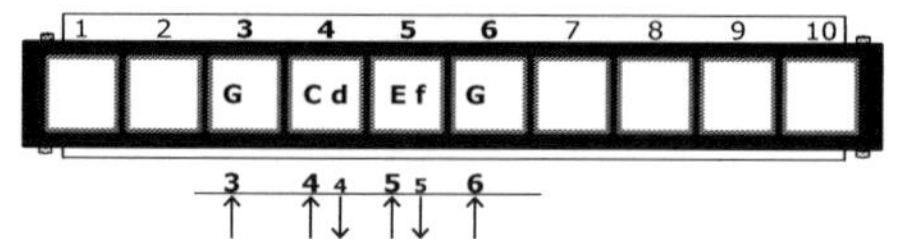

Joyful, Joyful

(We Adore Thee)

Blow = ↑ Draw = ↓

Large Number = BLOW
small number = draw

Classical

Ludwig Van Beethoven

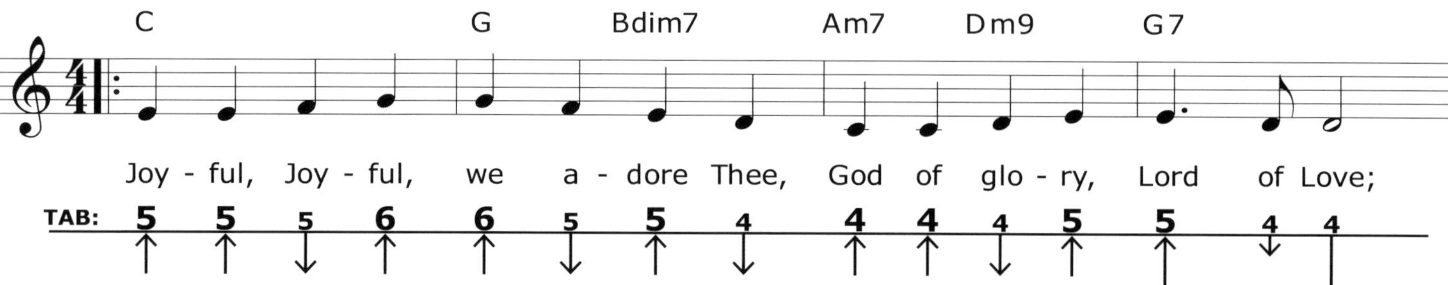

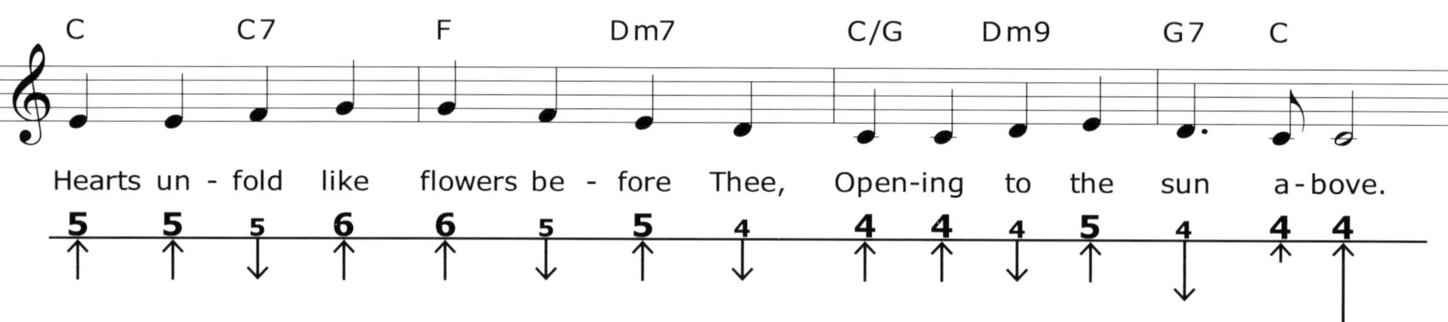

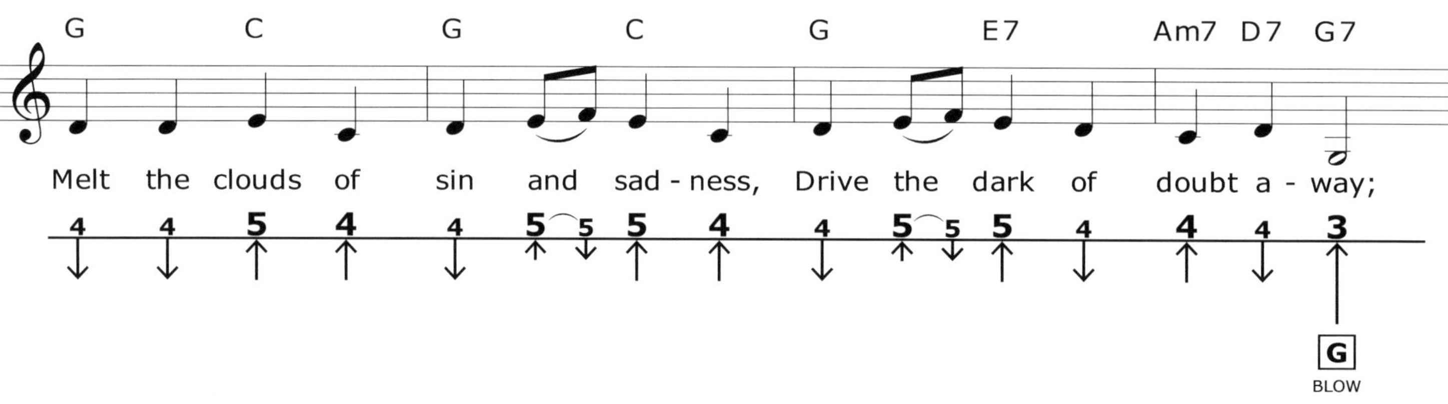

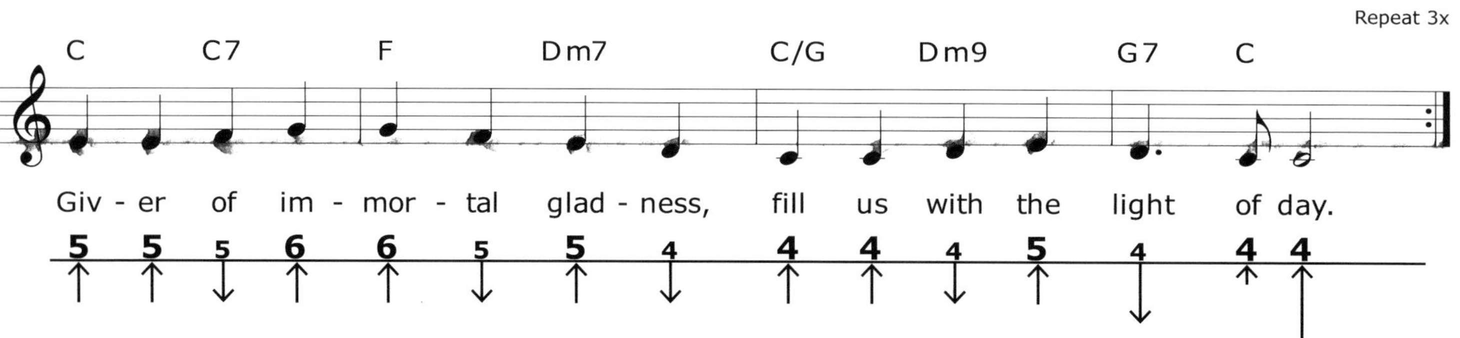

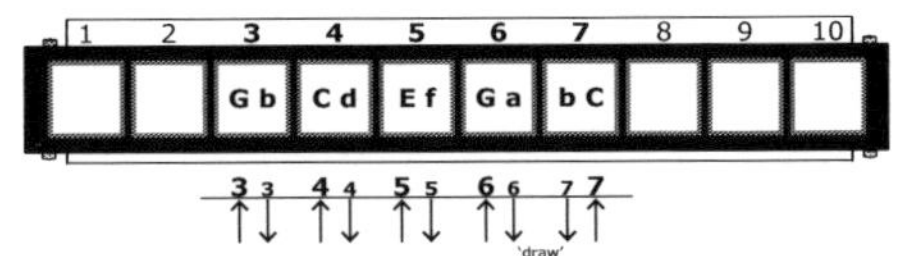

The Sloop John B.

Blow = ↑ Draw = ↓

Large Number = BLOW
small number = draw

Folk Country

Traditional

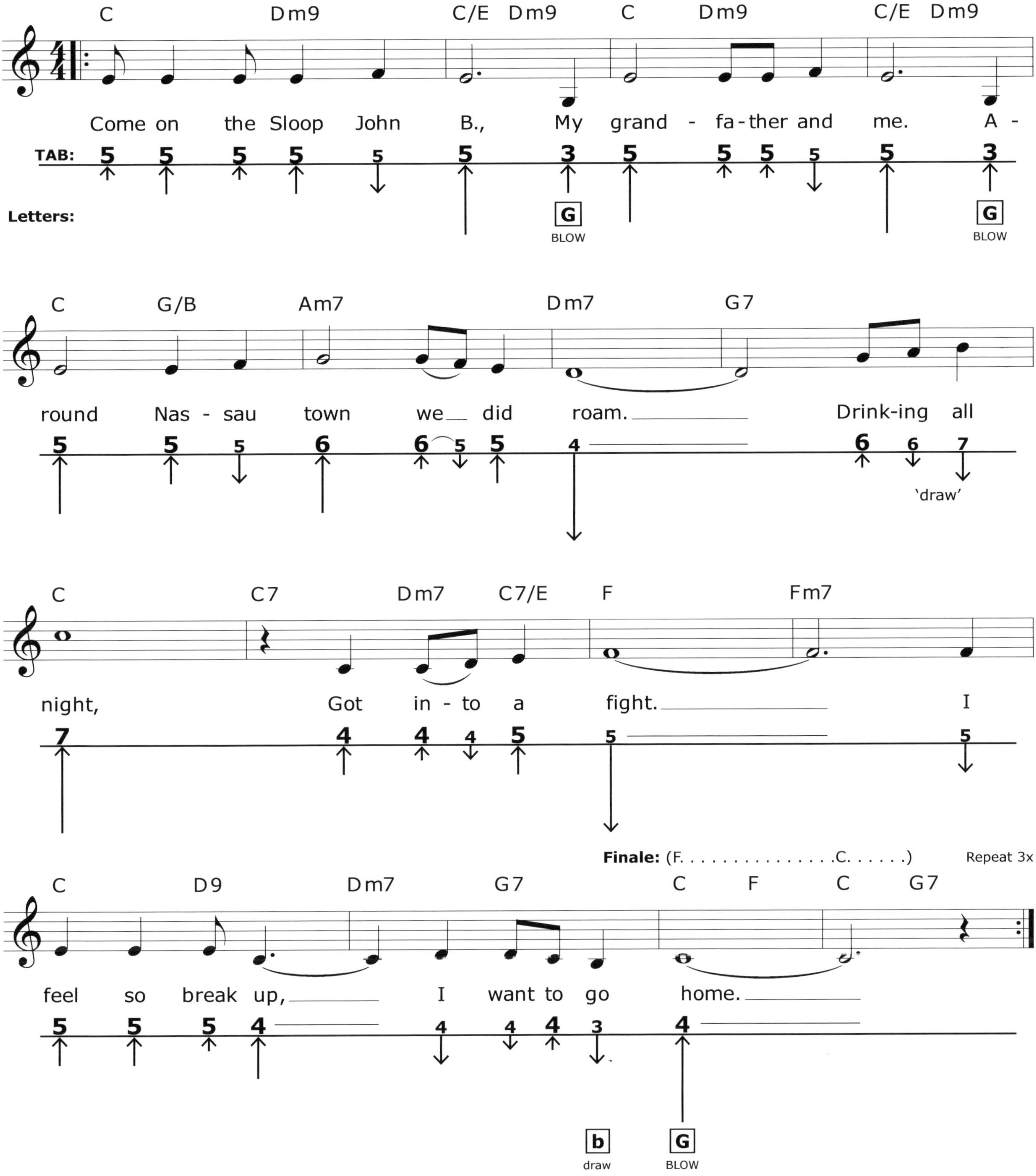

C Dm9 C/E Dm9 C Dm9 C/E Dm9

Come on the Sloop John B., My grand - fa-ther and me. A -

TAB: 5 5 5 5 5 5 3 5 5 5 5 5 3

Letters: G BLOW G BLOW

C G/B Am7 Dm7 G7

round Nas - sau town we did roam. Drink-ing all

5 5 5 6 6 5 5 4 6 6 7 'draw'

C C7 Dm7 C7/E F Fm7

night, Got in - to a fight. I

7 4 4 4 5 5 5

Finale: (F. . . . . .C. . . . . .) Repeat 3x

C D9 Dm7 G7 C F C G7

feel so break up, I want to go home.

5 5 5 4 4 4 4 3 4

b draw G BLOW

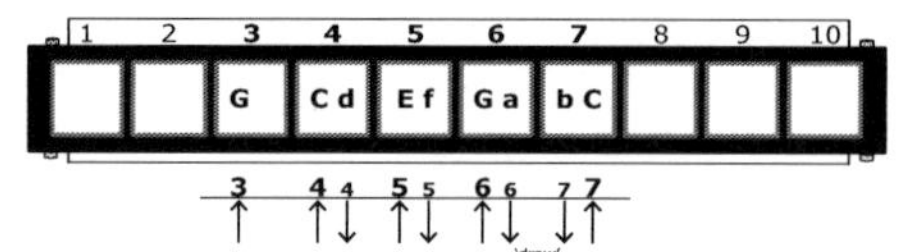

Oh, Shenandoah

Blow = ↑ Draw = ↓

Large Number = BLOW
small number = draw

Folk Country

Traditional

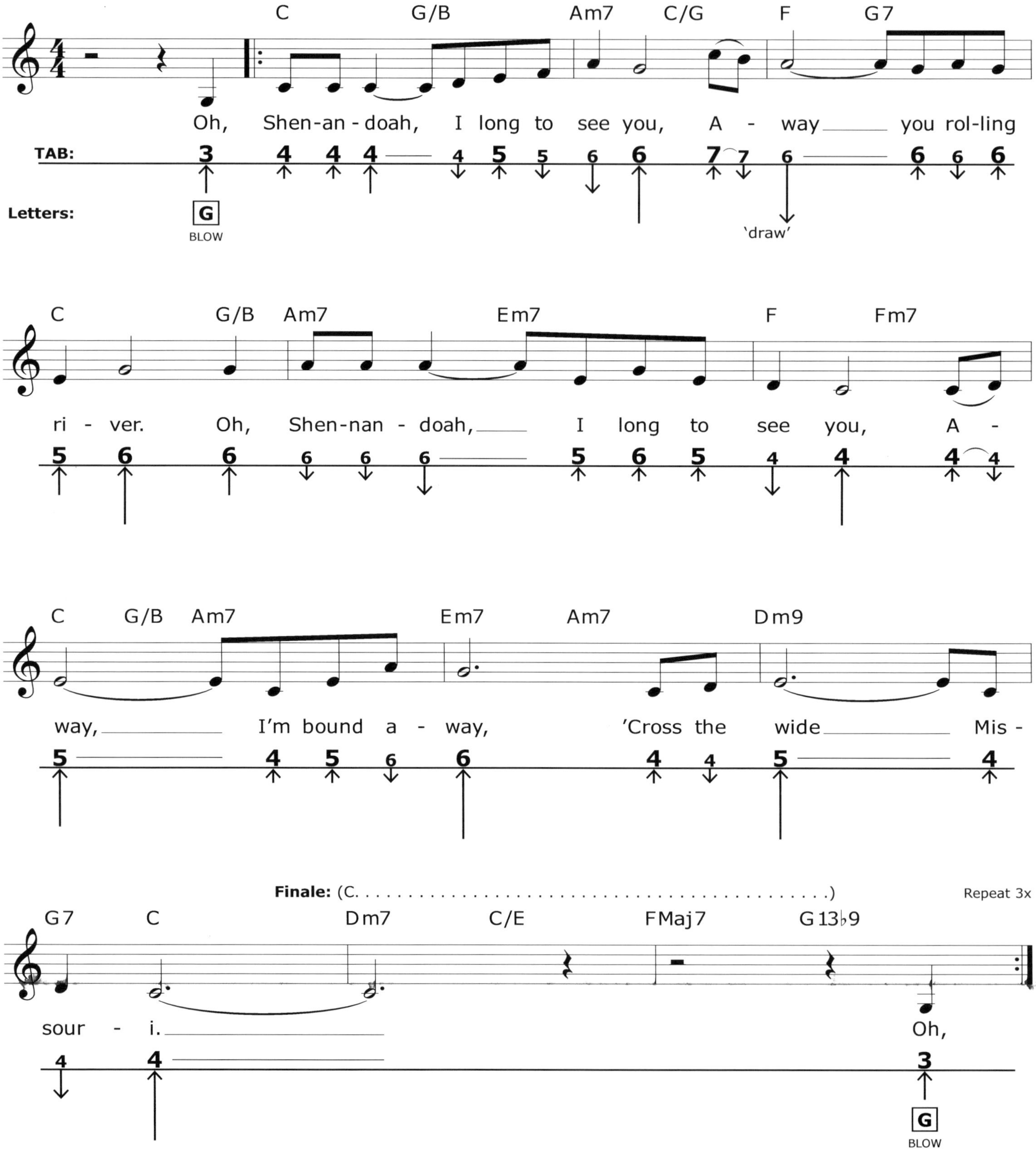

C G/B Am7 C/G F G7

Oh, Shen-an-doah, I long to see you, A - way ___ you rol-ling

TAB: 3 4 4 4 ___ 4 5 5 6 6 7 7 6 ___ 6 6 6

Letters: G BLOW 'draw'

C G/B Am7 Em7 F Fm7

ri - ver. Oh, Shen-nan - doah, ___ I long to see you, A -

5 6 6 6 6 6 ___ 5 6 5 4 4 4 4

C G/B Am7 Em7 Am7 Dm9

way, ___ I'm bound a - way, 'Cross the wide ___ Mis -

5 ___ 4 5 6 6 4 4 5 ___ 4

Finale: (C. . . . .) Repeat 3x

G7 C Dm7 C/E FMaj7 G13♭9

sour - i. ___ Oh,

4 4 ___ 3

G BLOW

CHAPTER 4

UPPER END OF THE HARMONICA

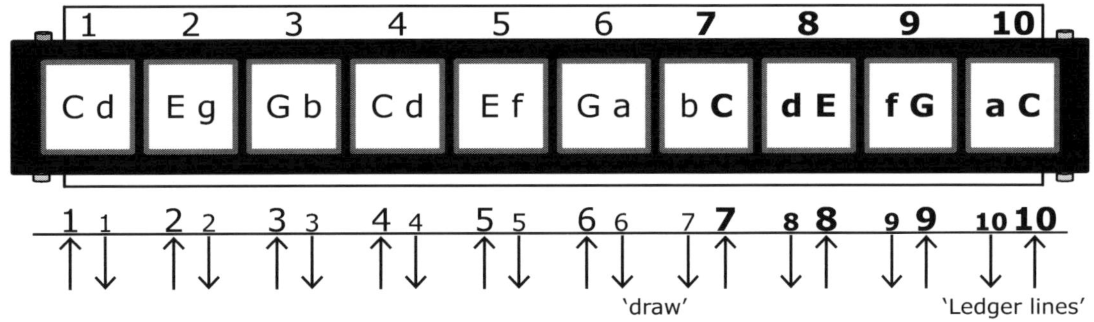

The upper tones require very little air.
However,
steady air pressure is necessary to carry or maintain the sound.

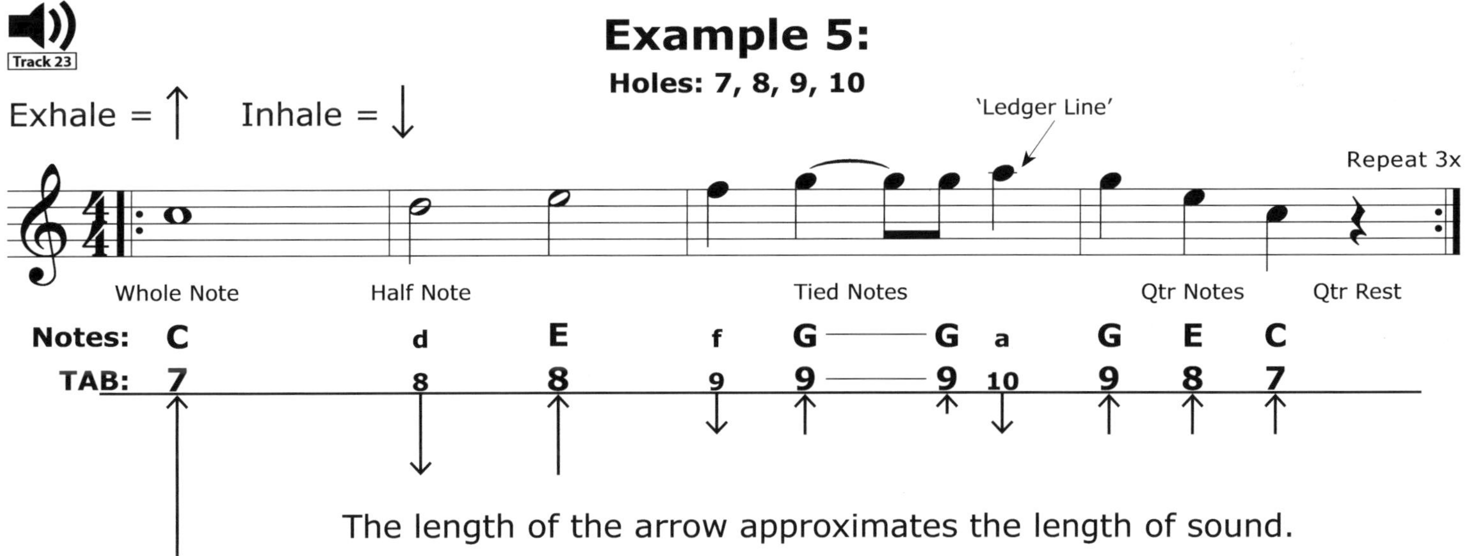

The length of the arrow approximates the length of sound.

Very seldom is blow 10, double high C, used for playing.
'**a**' and '**C**' are in hole 10. There is no '**b**' tone in the 10th hole.

Helpful Information:

In the early to Mid-20th century, folks who enjoyed harmonica usually played a G diatonic harmonica. The reasoning for this is that the G harmonica is pitched 4 tones lower than the C harmonica and uses the same tablature of numbers and arrows. The upper holes are easier to play on the G tuned harmonica. Using a G harmonica instead of a C harmonica for live performances might be considered on these next high-pitched tunes.

Along with the other notes on the harmonica,
the following tunes/songs will include:
Holes: 7, 8, 9, 10

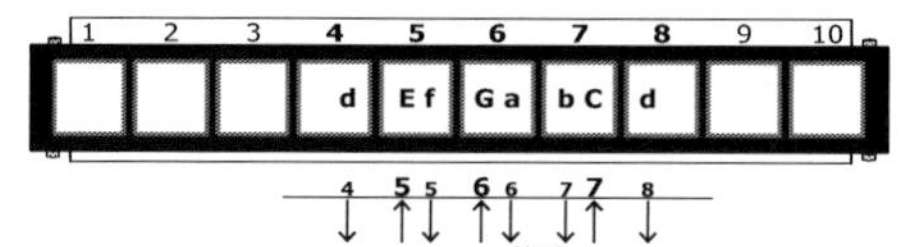

Scarborough Fair

Dorian Mode

Large Number = BLOW
small number = draw

Waltz

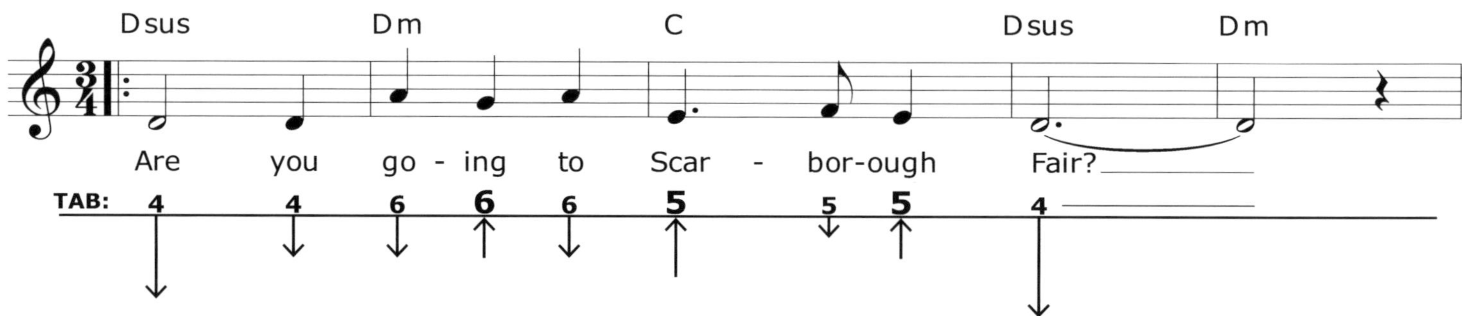

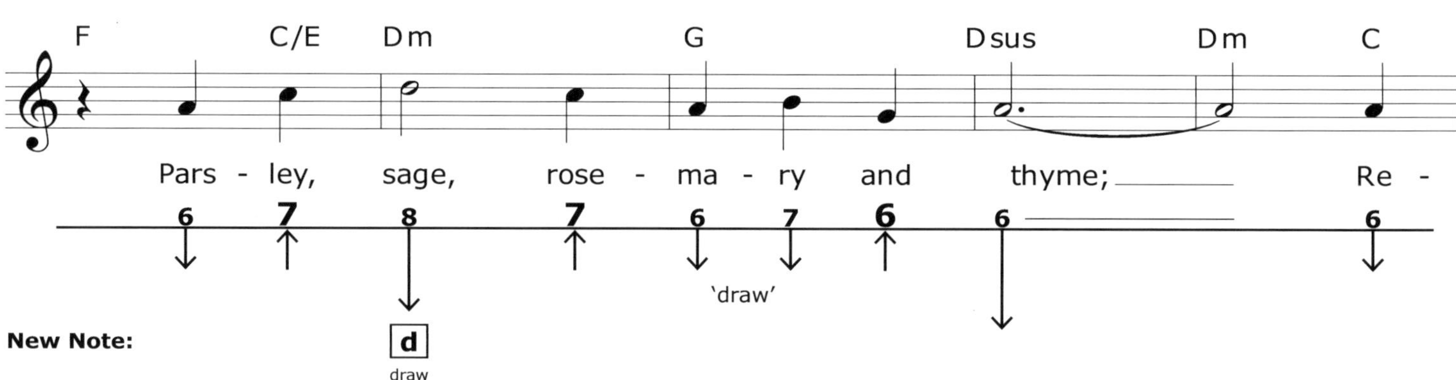

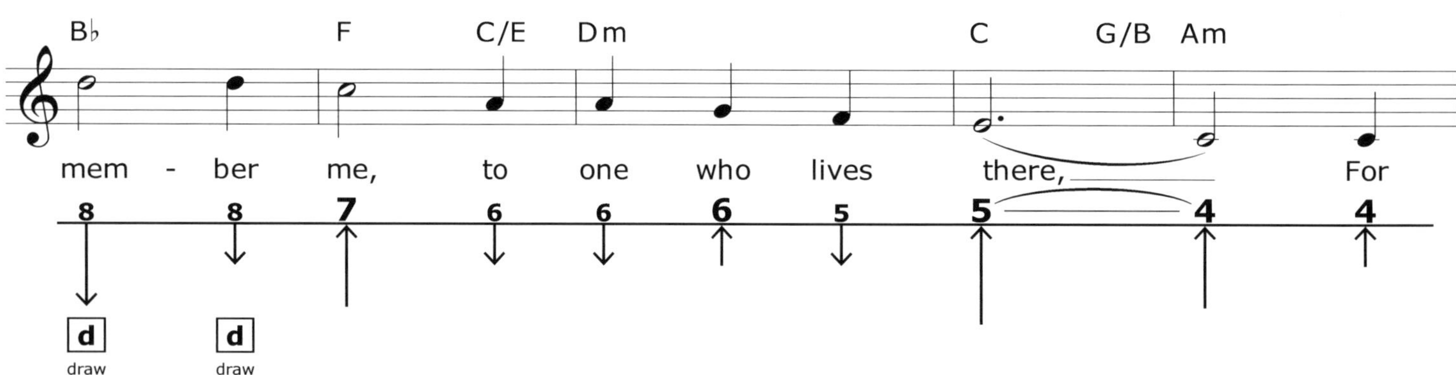

Finale: (Dm. . . . . . .) Repeat 3x

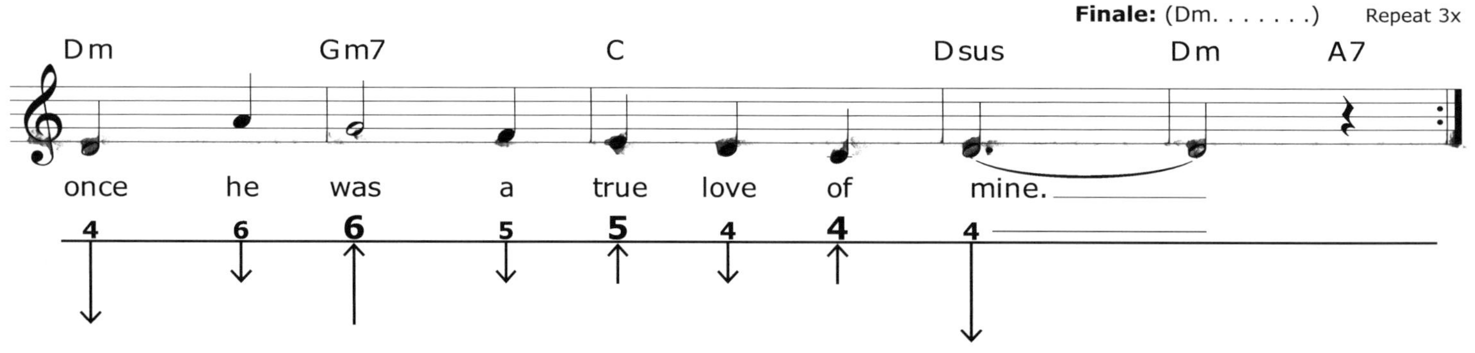

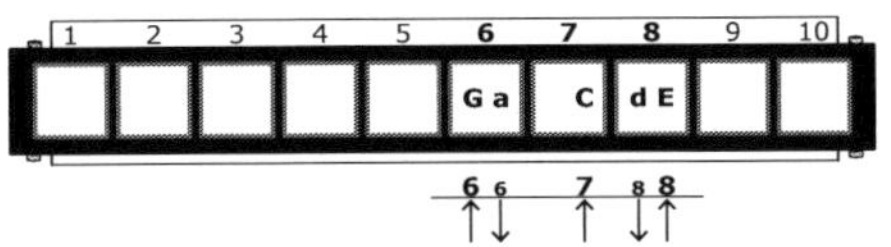

Lonesome Valley

Blow = ↑ Draw = ↓

Large Number = BLOW
small number = draw

Folk Music

Spiritual

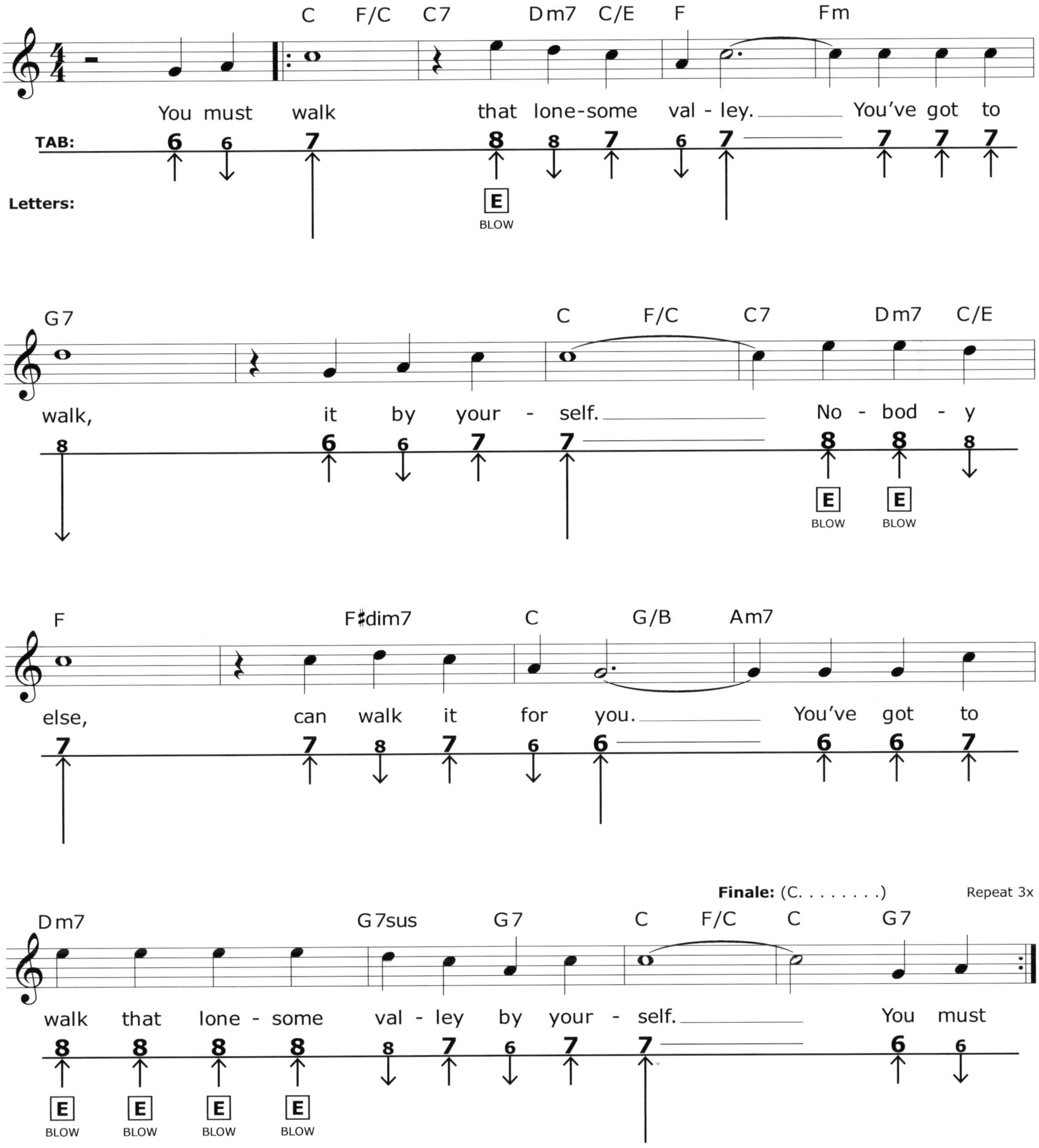

C F/C C7 Dm7 C/E F Fm

You must walk that lone-some val - ley. You've got to

TAB: 6↑ 6↓ 7↑ 8↑ 8↓ 7↑ 6↓ 7↑ 7↑ 7↑ 7↑

Letters: E BLOW

G7 C F/C C7 Dm7 C/E

walk, it by your - self. No - bod - y

8↓ 6↑ 6↓ 7↑ 7↑ 8↑ 8↑ 8↓

E BLOW E BLOW

F F♯dim7 C G/B Am7

else, can walk it for you. You've got to

7↑ 7↑ 8↓ 7↑ 6↓ 6↑ 6↑ 6↑ 7↑

Finale: (C. . . . .) Repeat 3x

Dm7 G7sus G7 C F/C C G7

walk that lone - some val - ley by your - self. You must

8↑ 8↑ 8↑ 8↑ 8↓ 7↑ 6↓ 7↑ 7↑ 6↑ 6↓

E BLOW E BLOW E BLOW E BLOW

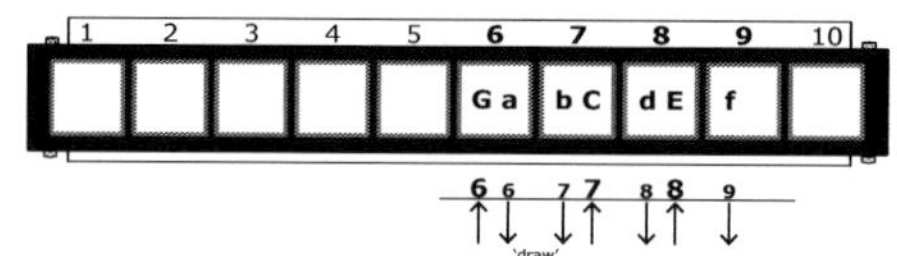

Aura Lee

Blow = ↑ Draw = ↓

Large Number = BLOW
small number = draw

Folk Music

Poulton/Fosdick

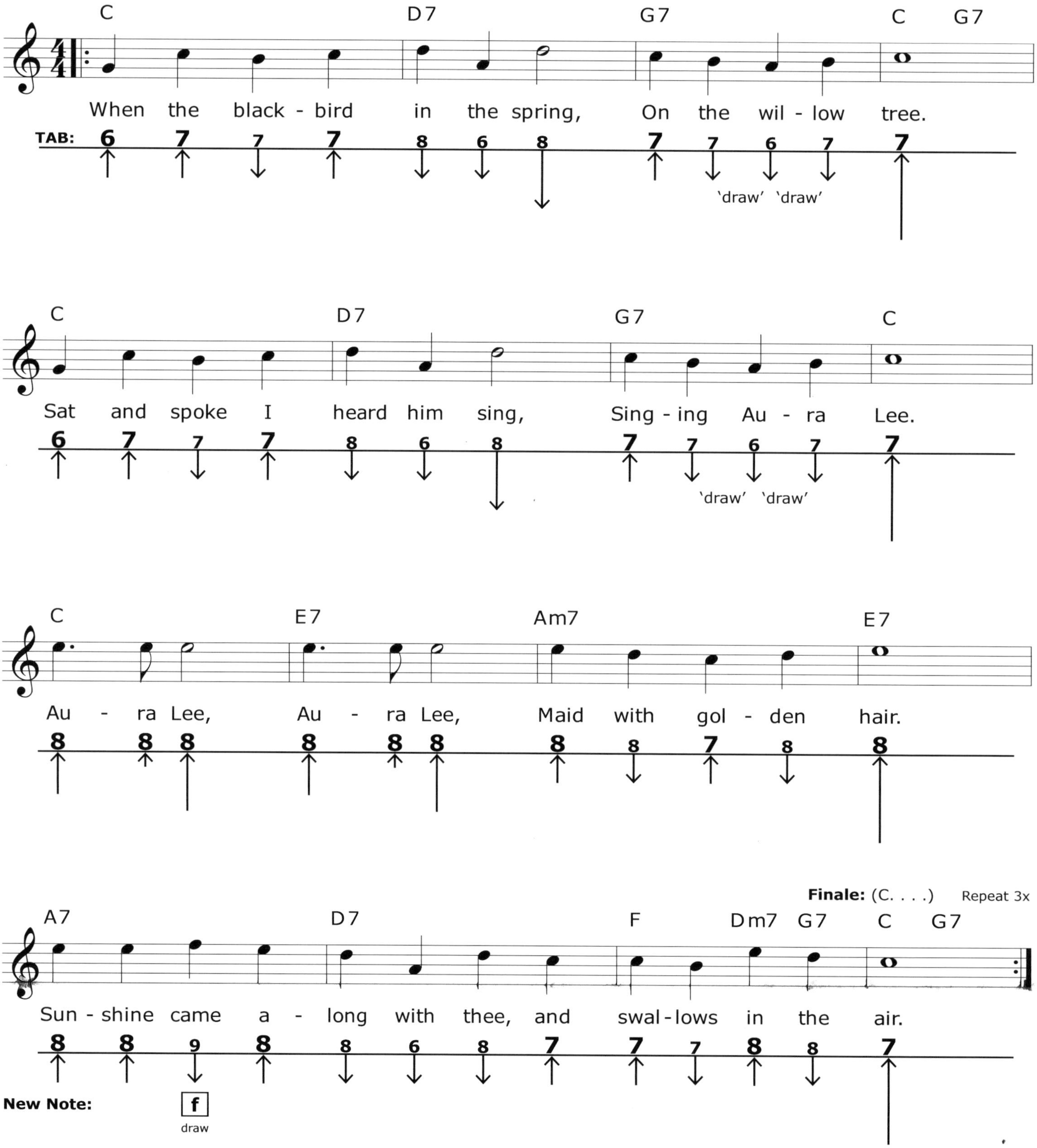

C D7 G7 C G7

When the black - bird in the spring, On the wil - low tree.

TAB: 6↑ 7↑ 7↓ 7↑ 8↓ 6↓ 8↓ 7↑ 7↓ 6↓ 7↓ 7↑

'draw' 'draw'

C D7 G7 C

Sat and spoke I heard him sing, Sing - ing Au - ra Lee.

6↑ 7↑ 7↓ 7↑ 8↓ 6↓ 8↓ 7↑ 7↓ 6↓ 7↓ 7↑

'draw' 'draw'

C E7 Am7 E7

Au - ra Lee, Au - ra Lee, Maid with gol - den hair.

8↑ 8↑ 8↑ 8↑ 8↑ 8↑ 8↑ 8↓ 7↑ 8↓ 8↑

Finale: (C. . . .) Repeat 3x

A7 D7 F Dm7 G7 C G7

Sun - shine came a - long with thee, and swal - lows in the air.

8↑ 8↑ 9↓ 8↑ 8↓ 6↓ 8↓ 7↑ 7↑ 7↓ 8↑ 8↓ 7↑

New Note: f draw

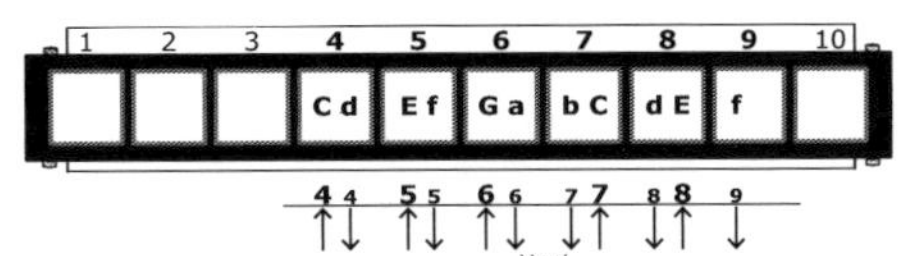

Silent Night

Large Number = BLOW
small number = draw

Franz Gerber (Gr.)

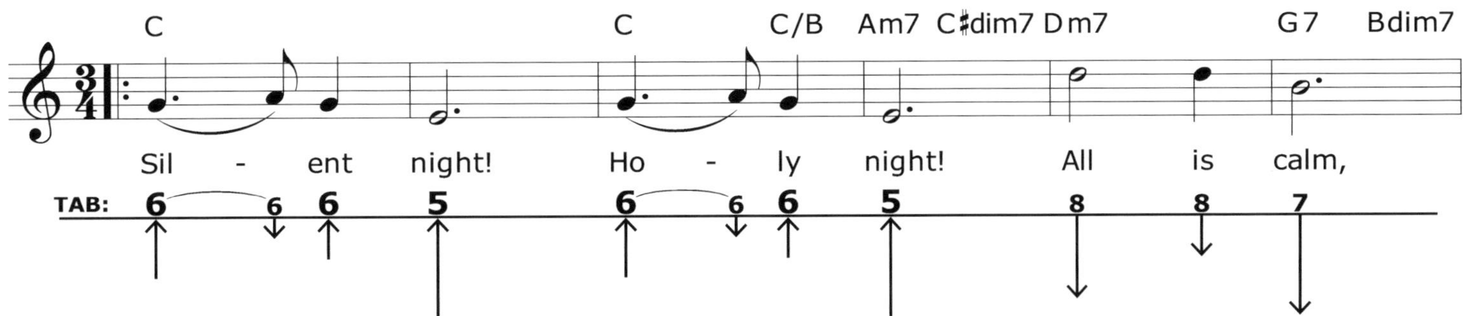

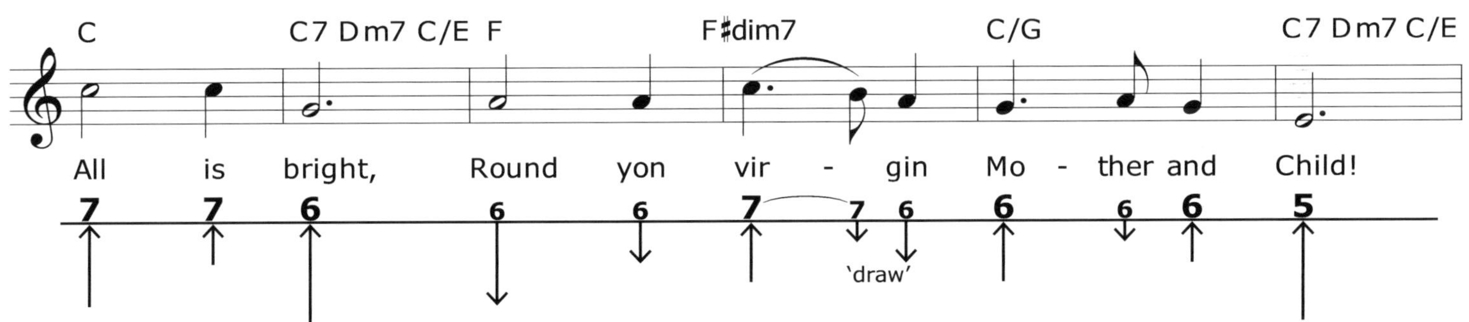

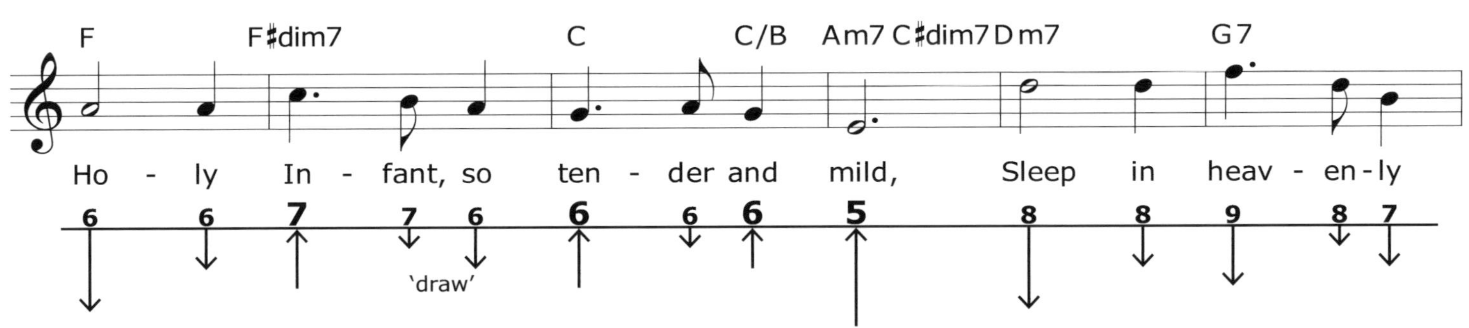

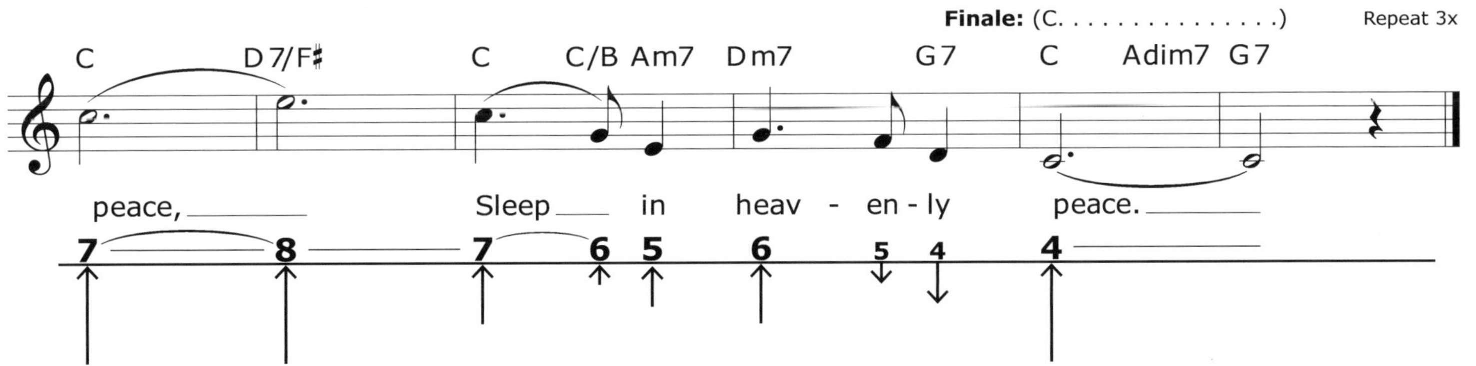

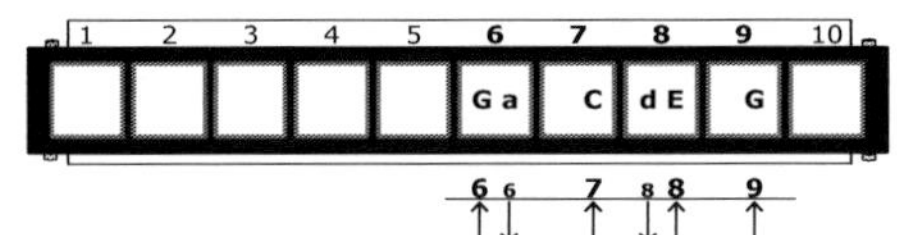

Amazing Grace

Blow = ↑ Draw = ↓

Large Number = BLOW
small number = draw

Gospel

John Newton

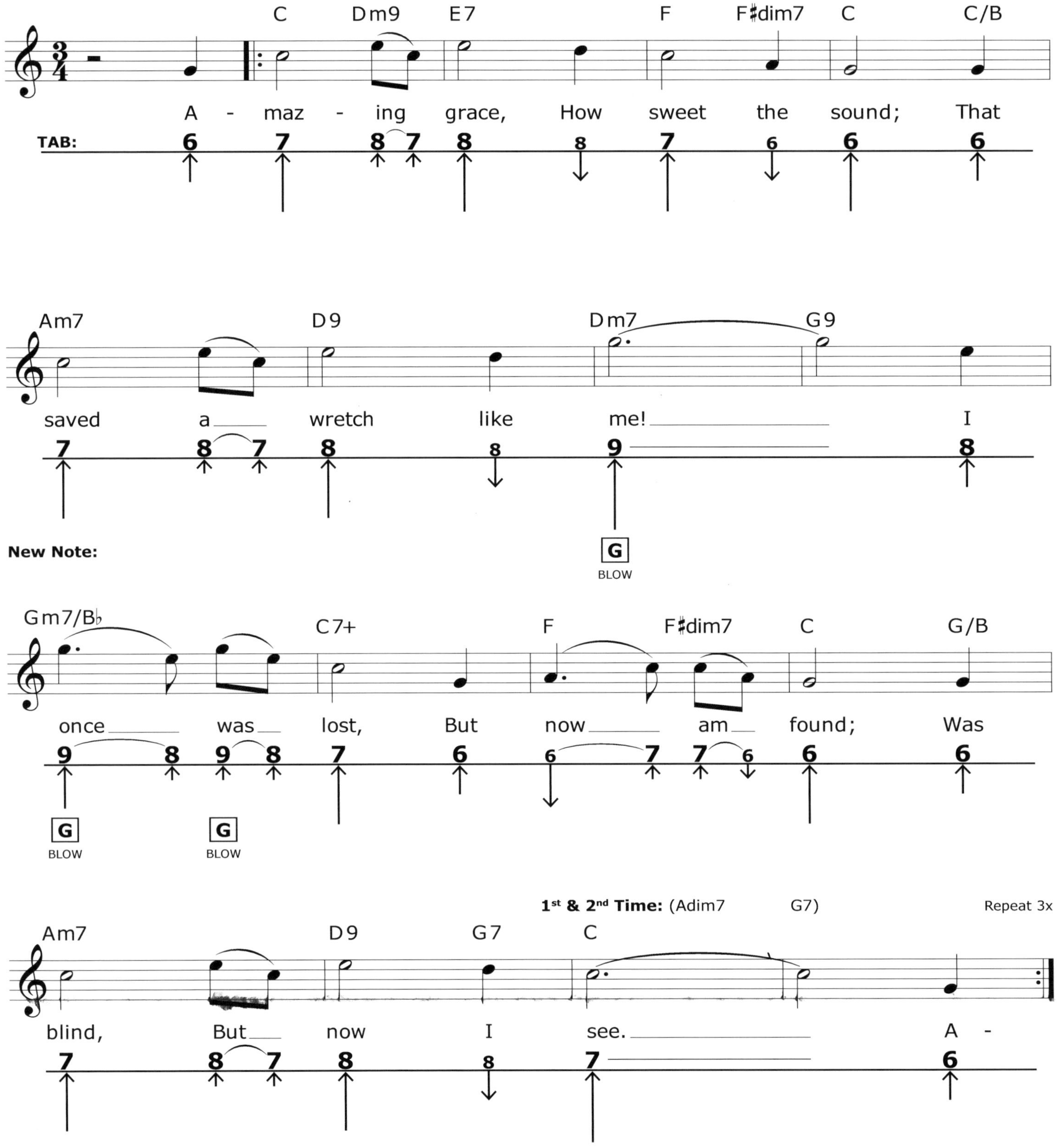

C Dm9 E7 F F♯dim7 C C/B

A - maz - ing grace, How sweet the sound; That

TAB: 6↑ 7↑ 8↑ 7↑ 8↑ 8↓ 7↑ 6↓ 6↑ 6↑

Am7 D9 Dm7 G9

saved a___ wretch like me!___ I

7↑ 8↑ 7↑ 8↑ 8↓ 9↑___ 8↑

New Note: G BLOW

Gm7/B♭ C7+ F F♯dim7 C G/B

once___ was___ lost, But now___ am___ found; Was

9↑ 8↑ 9↑ 8↑ 7↑ 6↑ 6↓ 7↑ 7↑ 6↓ 6↑ 6↑

G BLOW G BLOW

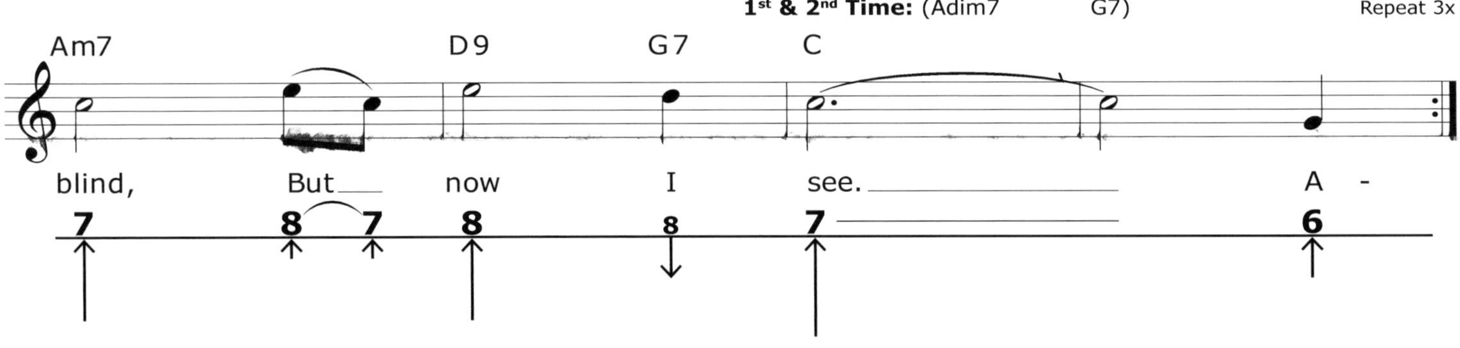

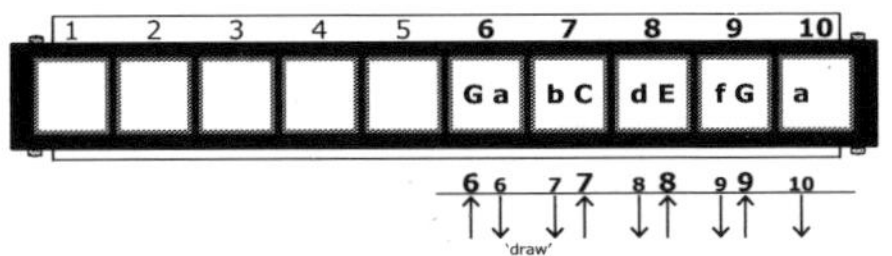

All Through the Night

Blow = ↑ Draw = ↓

Large Number = BLOW
small number = draw

Folk Music

Traditional

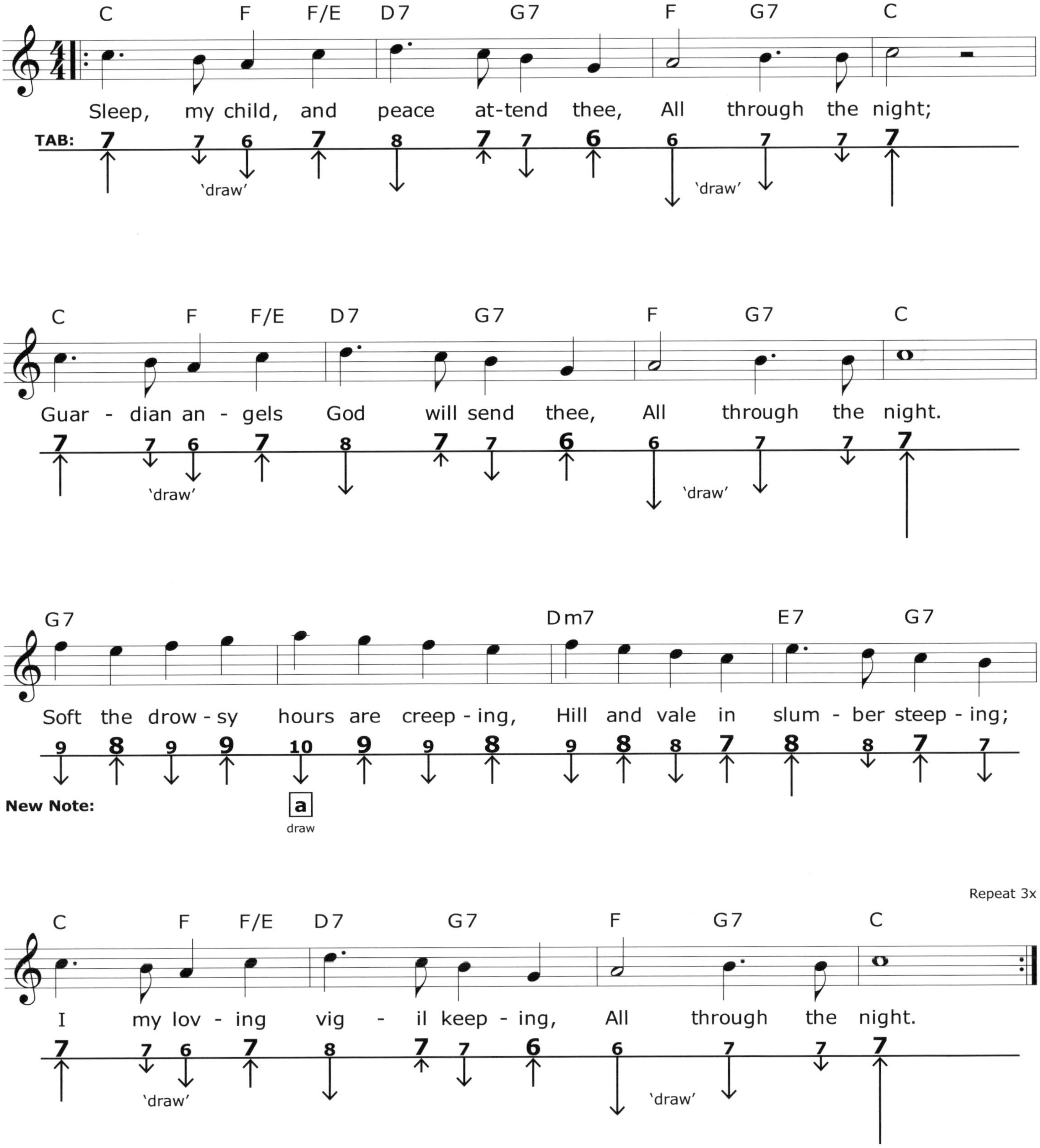

C F F/E D7 G7 F G7 C

Sleep, my child, and peace at-tend thee, All through the night;

TAB: 7 7 6 7 8 7 7 6 6 7 7 7

'draw' 'draw'

C F F/E D7 G7 F G7 C

Guar - dian an - gels God will send thee, All through the night.

7 7 6 7 8 7 7 6 6 7 7 7

'draw' 'draw'

G7 Dm7 E7 G7

Soft the drow - sy hours are creep - ing, Hill and vale in slum - ber steep - ing;

9 8 9 9 10 9 9 8 9 8 8 7 8 8 7 7

New Note: a draw

Repeat 3x

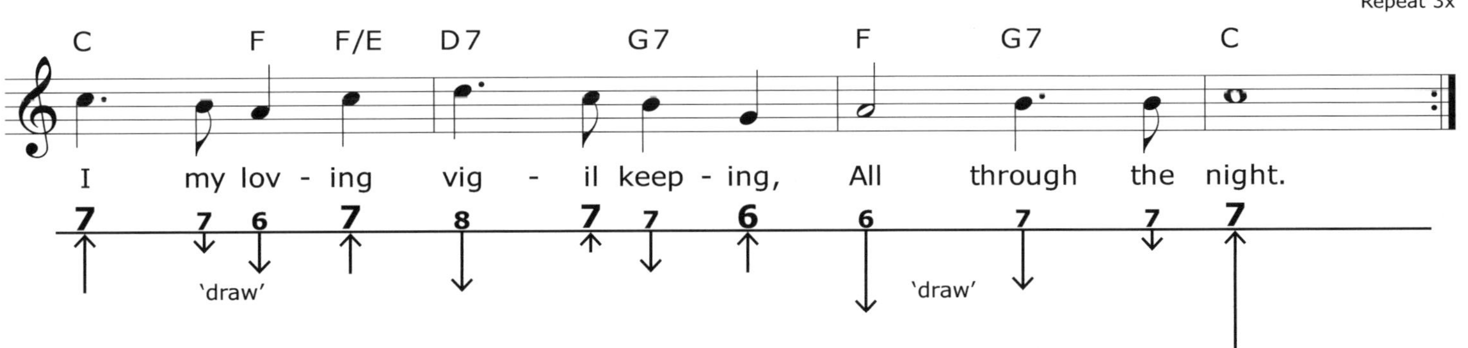

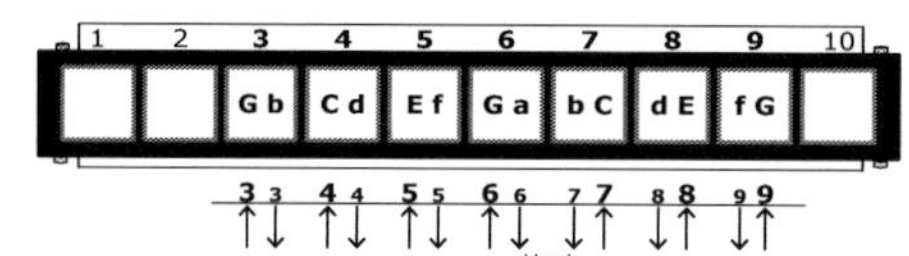

Home on the Range

Full Range: Lower, Middle and Upper Octaves

Large Number = BLOW
small number = draw

Folk Music

Cowboy

"**3**" counts to each measure

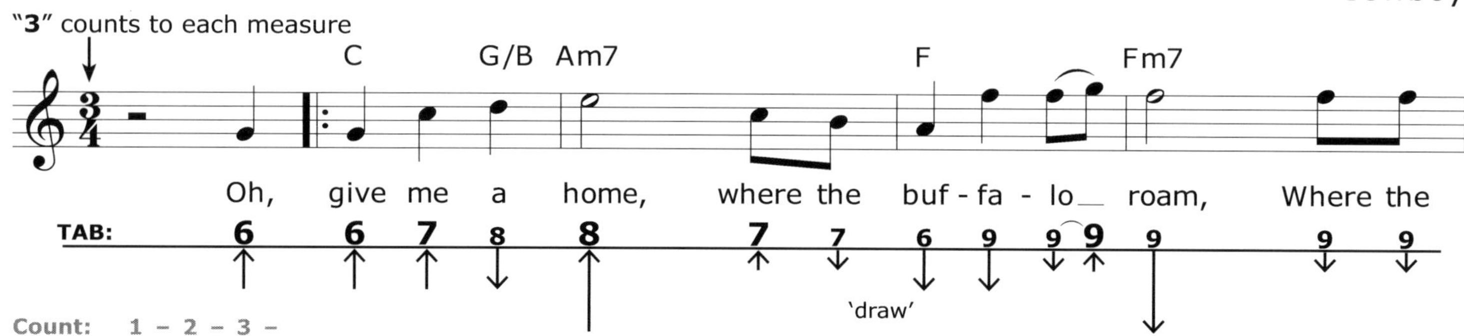

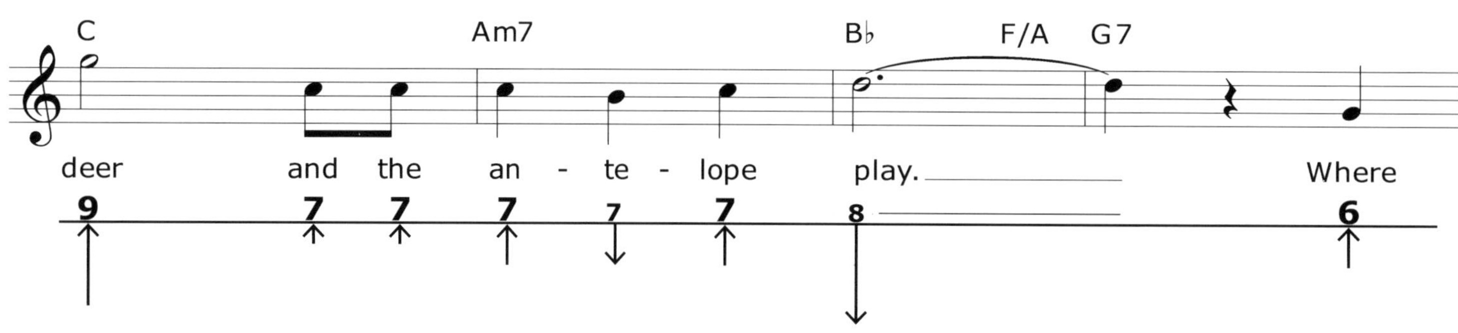

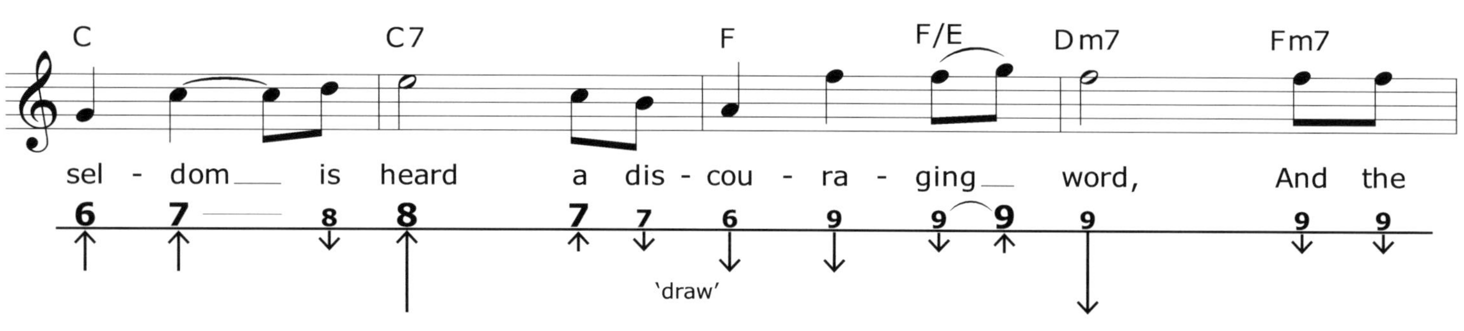

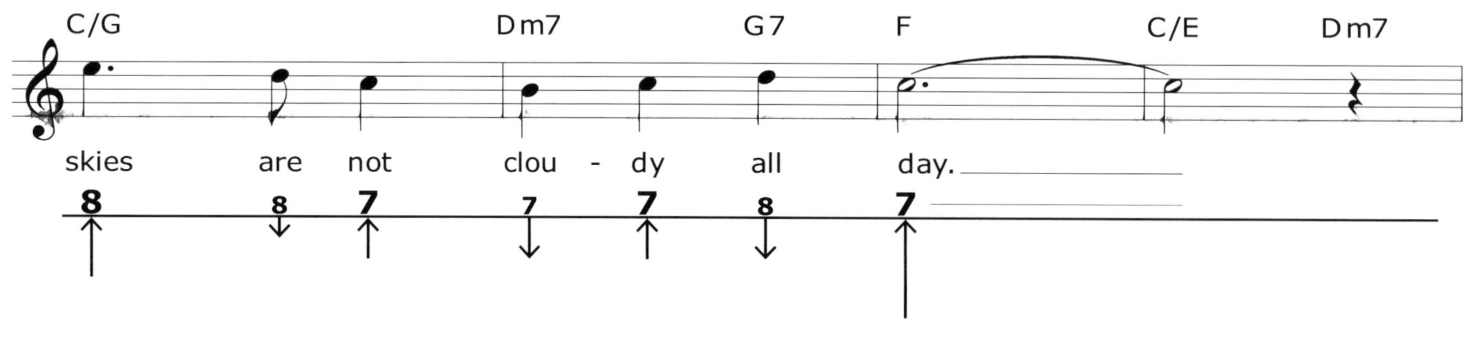

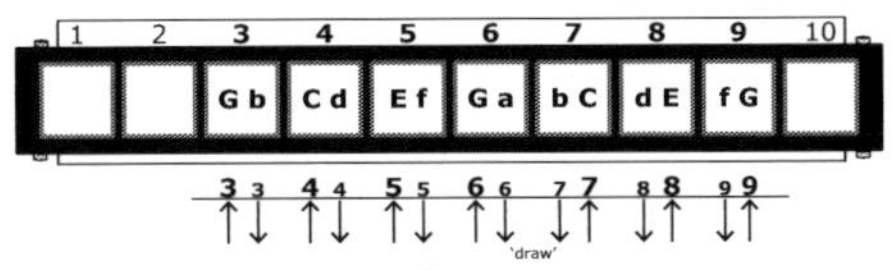

Home on the Range (Con't)

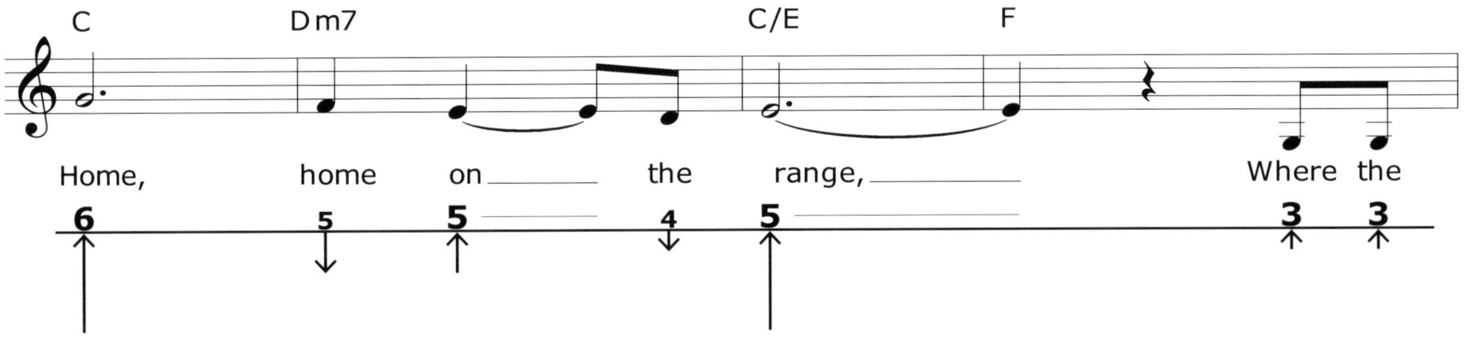

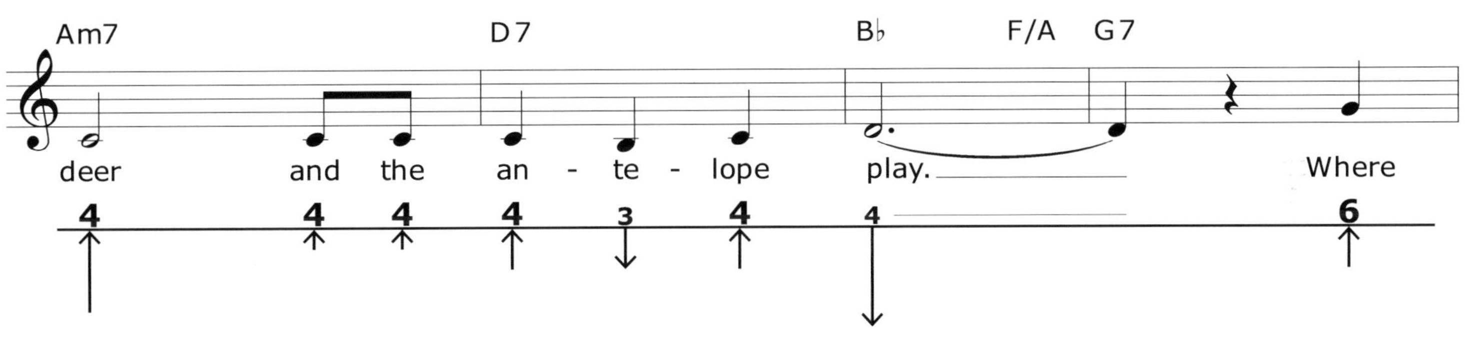

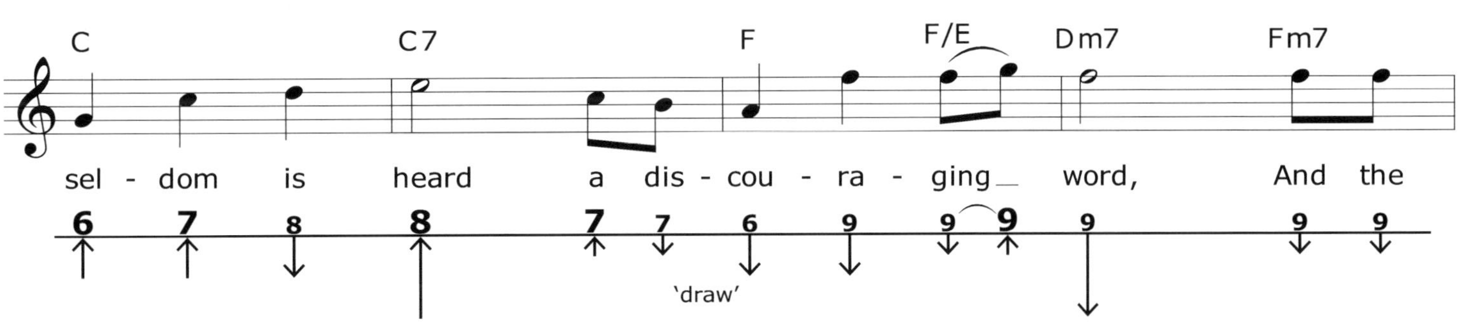

Finale: (C. . . . .) Repeat 3x

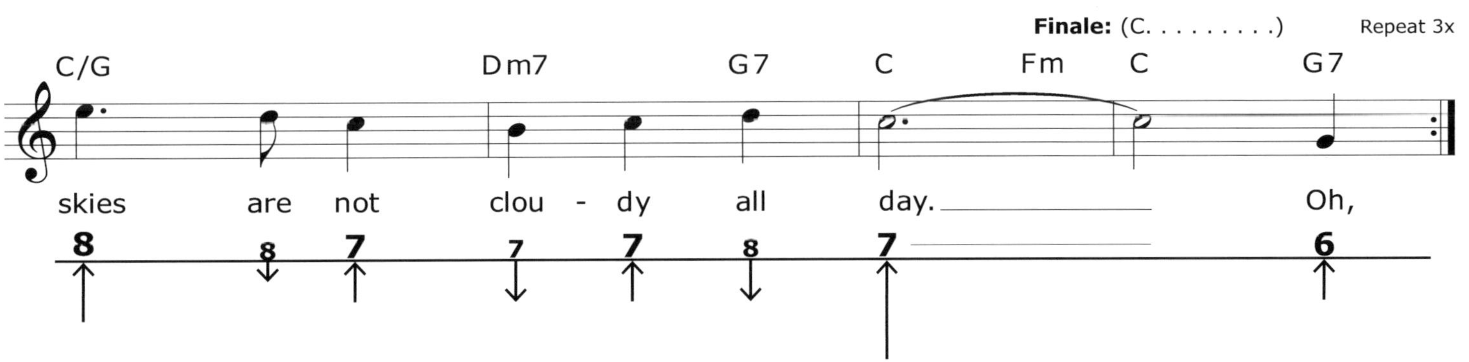

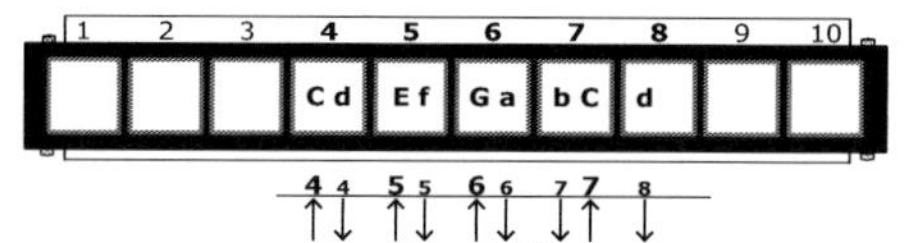

Walking Boogie

Large Number = BLOW
small number = draw

Blues

P. Duncan

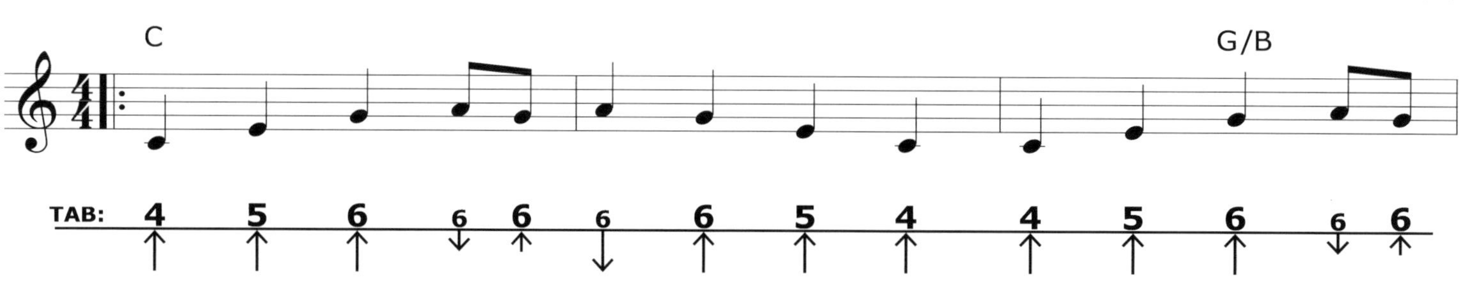

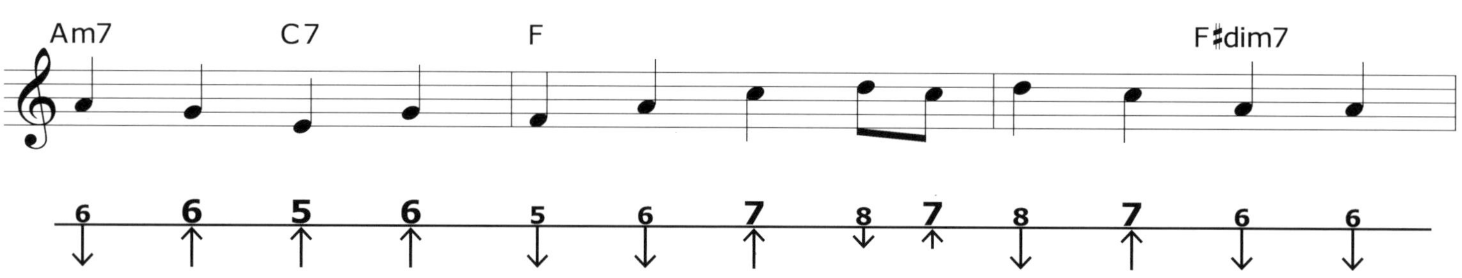

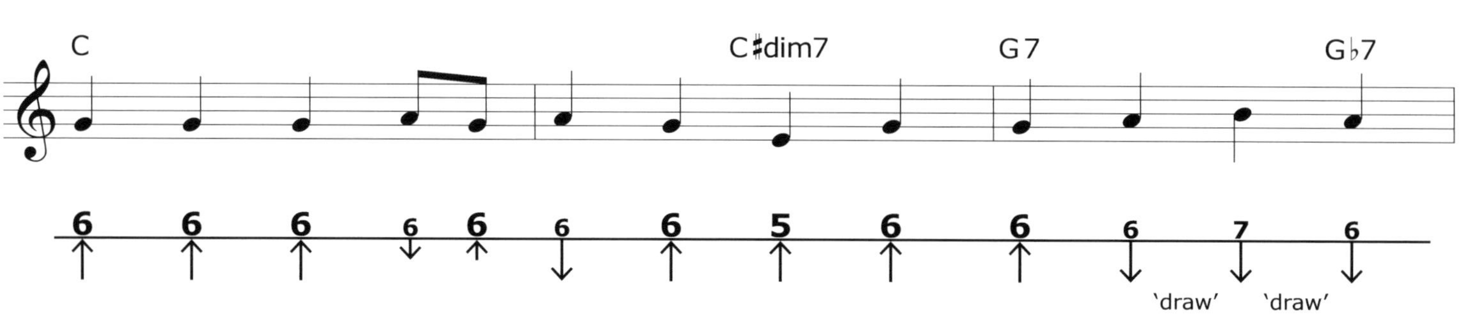

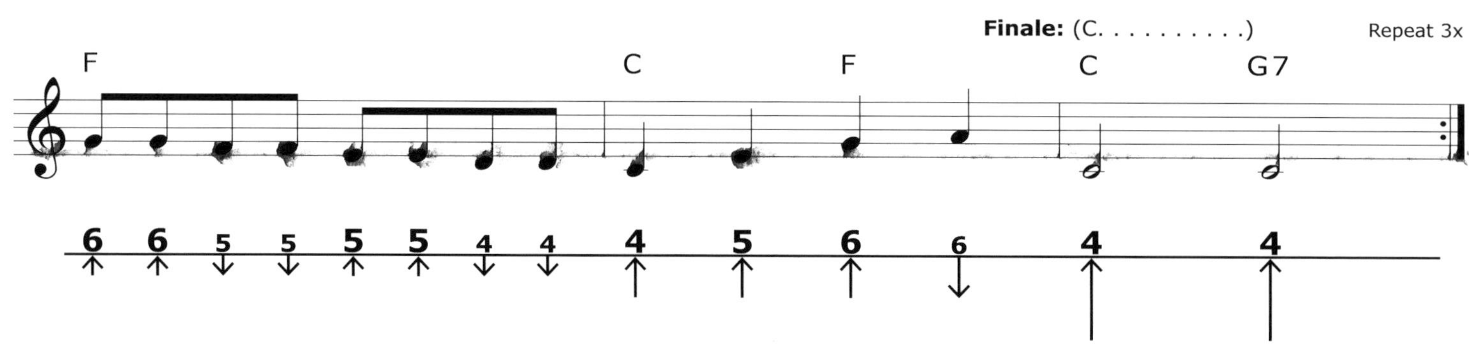

About the Author

At the age of seven, his grandfather taught him how to play the harmonica. He continued to play harmonica through high school, college and his military service. Upon returning to civilian life, he began to develop teaching procedures and methods for harmonica through adult community and public education.

Phil earned his Masters of Music Education degree in 1973 at the University of Missouri-Kansas City Conservatory of Music. His educator's experience ranged from elementary school through high school in the Park Hill School District in Kansas City, Missouri for 30 years. Later, he served as adjunct Professor at Park University in Parkville, Missouri as Director of Choral Music Activities for several years.

Mr. Duncan's career of 35 years as an author for Mel Bay Publications began in 1979. Since this beginning, Mel Bay has published over 33 instructional and music literature books for harmonica along with CD's and DVD's. He has written on virtually every aspect of playing the harmonica, making a significant contribution to the understanding and repertoire for this instrument.

MEL BAY